She s... ...t shot off.

Damn, he needed to stop reacting to her every time she smiled.

He touched her arm to stop her. "Shelby, about this morning. I need to apologize to you. I had no business kissing you."

She folded her arms across her chest. "I just thought you kissed all random women who come to your door."

He shook his head, then caught her mouth twitch. "Not random women, only beautiful women with big blue eyes who appear at my back door at five in the morning."

She cocked her head and desire shot through him again. "Cullen, I can't have a relationship right now." She glanced away. "My life has to be focused on Ryan."

He held up a hand. "I feel the same way. I'm only here for a few months. My job isn't even permanent."

She laughed. "Well, with all those complications, I'd say we don't have to worry."

HER COLORADO SHERIFF

BY
PATRICIA THAYER

First Published in Great Britain 2017
By Mills & Boon, an imprint of HarperCollins*Publishers*
1 London Bridge Street, London, SE1 9GF

© 2017 Patricia Wright

ISBN: 978-0-263-92267-7

23-0117

Our policy is to use papers that are natural, renewable and recyclable products and made from wood grown in sustainable forests. The logging and manufacturing processes conform to the legal environmental regulations of the country of origin.

Printed and bound in Spain
by CPI, Barcelona

Patricia Thayer was born and raised in Muncie, Indiana, the second in a family of eight children. She attended Ball State University before heading west, where she has called Southern California home for many years. There she's been a member of the Orange County Chapter of RWA. It's a sisterhood like no other.

When not working on a story, she might be found traveling the United States and Europe, taking in the scenery and doing story research while enjoying time with her husband, Steve. Together, they have three grown sons and four grandsons and one granddaughter, whom Patricia calls her own true-life heroes.

As always, Steve.
And to the next 45 years together.

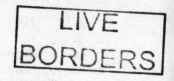
Chapter One

With a gasp, Shelby Townsend sat up in bed, her room dark and foreboding. The tree blowing in the wind outside her window cast ominous shadows on her wall. She ignored her own fears when she heard the child's cry again.

"Ryan." She jumped up and hurried across the hall into the other bedroom. There she found the five-year-old boy thrashing around on the single bed.

She sat down on the mattress and grabbed his flaying arms. "Ryan, it's okay. I'm here," she whispered in what she hoped was a soothing voice. "Aunt Shelby is here."

The child's cries and fighting stopped as the blond-haired boy opened his eyes. He made an indistinguishable sound as he gripped her hands tightly. "Aunt Shellie. The bad man is going to get me. I'm scared."

"I know, but I won't let anyone hurt you."

The boy sat up and hugged her. "I want Mama," he cried.

"I know, Ryan. I know."

Shelby's heart tightened painfully, making it hard to breathe. How could she explain to this child that his mother wasn't going to come back? Ever. Ryan wouldn't understand the awful things that happened only two weeks ago. How could he? Even she didn't understand why her big sister had been killed.

"I want… I want to go home."

This was to be expected since it was the first night in their new home. Ryan didn't handle change well.

She rubbed his back, hoping to calm him. They could never go back to Kentucky. Besides, there wasn't anything left there to return for.

Tears filled her eyes as she remembered the events of the past few weeks. She was running late from picking Ryan up from school. If only she'd convinced Georgia to come with her instead of meeting them… Things might have turned out differently, and she'd still have a sister, and her nephew would have his mother.

"I'm sorry, Ryan, but we can't go back there. This is our home now." At least for the next few months, they'd be hidden out here in the country, until branding season was over.

Shelby almost laughed at the situation. The small town of Hidden Springs, Colorado, was a funny place for a sous-chef to end up.

The town was chosen not because of her culinary skills, but the best area for them to find a safe place to settle in, and create a new life. For now, the large Circle R Ranch was a good hideout.

Ryan raised his head. "Please, can I have the tablet?"

She knew that she shouldn't give in, but the child needed something to calm him after the bad dream. She went to the desk and retrieved the device. After putting on a timer, she handed it to him. "You can look at your pictures for twenty minutes only."

She was rewarded with a rare smile. She kissed the boy and left the room. Too keyed up to go back to sleep, she slipped on her robe over her flannel pajama bottoms and tank top, then headed down the stairs in the cozy farmhouse.

Once on the main floor, she glanced at the sheet-covered furniture in the living room, reminding her of the cleaning job she had tomorrow. She was a little curious as to why no one was here to meet them. She also had to search for the key, and found it over the door, then let herself inside. She was still wondering if Georgia had been confused about the living arrangements.

Shelby continued through the dining room, filled with a long table and hutch. Who would use this place for temporary employees? It had been Georgia who'd found the ad for a roundup cook online. Room and board was included, and the job was far enough away from Dawkins Meadow to hopefully keep Gil Bryant out of their lives.

A shiver ran through her body as she glanced out the big windows over the sink and into the moon-bright night. No streetlights out here on the ranch. She filled the kettle and took it to the stove, hoping some chamomile tea would help her sleep. But in her heart, she knew that it would take a long time before she could rid herself of the nightmare of the few past weeks. And the terrible death of her sister would never go away.

Now her goal was to move ahead with her life and keep Ryan safe.

HE BLAMED IT on the full moon.

Cullen Brannigan drove his patrol car off the highway onto the county road leading to the ranch. His sour mood had nothing to do with driving through the small community of Hidden Springs, and the outlying areas.

He should have his head examined for taking this interim sheriff's position. *Thank you, Trent, for talking me into this.*

After chasing down high school seniors who'd played pranks on unsuspecting residents, tearing a new pair of uniform pants, he was rethinking his decision to accept the job here.

He wasn't a small-town sheriff. He was a Denver police detective. At least he had been before he was suspected of taking bribes while working white-collar crimes one year ago. While Internal Affairs investigated leads, he'd been suspended from the force. Even though he'd been cleared and reinstated, he wasn't sure he could go back. As if his fellow officers would ever trust him again.

That went both ways. The brotherhood hadn't exactly stood up for him during the investigation, either, but his father's betrayal had been the worst. Captain Neal Brannigan couldn't possibly have taken his son's word of his innocence. Maybe his stepbrother, Trent, was right; a fresh start was what he needed to move on.

Cullen shook away the memories as he turned his vehicle onto the gravel road, the bright moonlight showing him the way. Damn, it was pitch-black out here in the sticks. And for now, thanks to his recently deceased stepmother, Leslie Landry Brannigan, he owned part of these sticks. Part of a ranch, to be exact.

Maybe it was time he had a look at his new home, especially since he'd gotten a radio call saying that a passing neighbor had seen an unfamiliar car in the driveway. For years, the property had been leased out, but with his stepmother's death, the land transferred to her sons. So the renters were notified and had moved out of the guest cottage two weeks ago. The place should be deserted.

Cullen drove under the wrought iron sign that read Circle R Ranch. Leslie had told him many stories about her parents' large cattle operation back in the day. Until her sudden death last month, he had no idea that she'd willed the place to him, his twin brother, Austin, and her biological son, Trent. The property was to be divided between them equally. He guessed Leslie wanted her boys to know she loved them equally.

Damn, he missed her.

He drove past the faded red barn and into the driveway at the front of her house. The Victorian structure needed a lot of work, but she was still grand to look at. He got out of the patrol car and walked around the side of the house where he spotted the small sedan parked in the driveway. He glanced at the dim light in the kitchen.

He walked back out front as he punched Trent's number into his phone. He knew it was late, but he wanted to double-check if he'd been expecting anyone here.

He got a groggy greeting. "Hello, Cullen. What's going on?"

"I'm over at your grandfather Robertson's place. There's a car parked here." He rambled off the make and model and plates. "Do you know them?"

"They could be related to the Donaldsons, who just moved out."

"Could they get into the main house?"

He heard a sigh. "To be honest, Cullen, I'm not sure. I haven't been there in years. All the rent money went to Mom."

"Okay, then I'll see if I can stir someone."

"Hey, give me a few minutes, and I'll be there to help you."

"I don't need a big brother anymore," he teased, recalling their intense days as teenagers. "I'll knock on the door, and if there's anything suspect, I'll call for backup."

Cullen hung up and climbed the steps to the front door. He rang the bell, then a minute later with no answer, he began to knock hard on the door and called out.

He unfastened the strap on his gun. "Sheriff's department. Please, open the door."

SHELBY FROZE. Oh, God, no. Gil had found them. She stood and hurried into the other room. What should she do? She rushed to the window and peeked out through the heavy curtains. She found a tall, well-built stranger standing under the porch light. She glanced toward the black-and-white car with the logo of County Sheriff on the side.

The knock sounded again. "Who's ever inside, you need to answer the door. You are trespassing on private property."

She heard Ryan's loud cry from upstairs. She ran to the stairs and called to her nephew. "Go back to your room, Ryan. It's okay."

When the boy disappeared, Shelby took a shaky breath and released it. She stood by the door. "What do you want, Sheriff?"

"Would you please step out on the porch? I need to speak to you."

With trembling hands, she unbolted the door, but left the chain on, then opened it a crack to see the dark-haired man in uniform. Well, if you could call dark jeans, boots and a light blue shirt a uniform. Around his waist he wore a gun, and several other weapons.

"May I see your identification, Sheriff?"

He looked irritated, but pulled out an official ID. She read the name Cullen Brannigan. He was six feet one inch tall, his weight one hundred ninety, eyes, hazel, and hair, brown.

"Thank you." She handed it back to him. "I'm not trespassing, Sheriff. I was hired to come here and cook for spring roundup. The job came with room and board."

He frowned. "Who hired you?"

"The Donaldson family."

He nodded. "May I see your identification?"

"Of course." Shelby went to the table next to the door and got her wallet. She didn't want to bring attention to herself. If Gil got news of her being here with a computer search… "All you have to do is contact Mr. Donaldson. He'll tell you that we're supposed to be here. But he talked with my sister, Georgia Hughes." That had been what her new ID stated. She was supposed to have a chance to start over. She handed over her Kentucky driver's license. "If there is a mistake, we'll leave."

"Where is your sister?"

Miss Townsend glanced away. "She died unexpectedly… We just recently buried her before we came here."

Before she could say any more, a truck pulled up into the yard. Shelby stiffened and pulled her robe closer to her body as another man climbed out and rushed up to the porch.

"Hey, bro." He turned that smile toward Shelby. "Hello, I'm Trent Landry."

"I'm Shelby Townsend. I was just explaining to the sheriff, my sister and I were hired to cook for the roundup for Mr. Donaldson."

Trent nodded. "I'm sorry, but the Donaldsons no longer live here. Since my mother's passing, this property has changed hands. I'm surprised you haven't been contacted by Hank."

Shelby tried to stay calm given this new situation. Oh, God. Now, what was she going to do? "We were probably on the road by then." Had Georgia known the change of plans and never got the chance to tell her? "I apologize for the mistake." She opened the door and allowed both men inside. "As you can see, nothing was disturbed. We only arrived a few hours ago."

Cullen watched as the attractive brunette fidgeted with the belt on her robe. Something told him she wasn't telling him the entire story. He glanced around at the large room filled with sheet-covered furniture. The place was huge.

The woman started to speak when a child's voice rang out from upstairs. "It's okay, Ryan," she said. "You can come downstairs."

A little boy about five hurried down the steps and ran to her side. He looked scared, and Cullen hated that he'd caused the boy any more stress.

Trent spoke first. "Hello, there. I'm Trent. What's your name?"

The boy looked up at his aunt. "It's Ryan," she said for him. "He's five."

"Good to meet you, Ryan," Trent said. "Sorry if we scared you."

"Don't hurt Aunt Shellie," he said slowly.

The woman stepped in. "No one is going to hurt anyone, Ryan. This is Sheriff Cullen."

The boy's eyes widened before he buried his head against his aunt's waist.

"He's very shy and a little frightened. I apologize for the mistake. If you give us about thirty minutes we can be packed up and out of here."

Hell, he didn't want to kick her out onto the street. Cullen spoke up. "Whoa, we aren't kicking you out in the middle of the night."

OUTSIDE THE HOUSE, Trent asked, "So you think it's okay to let them stay?"

Cullen still wasn't sure what came over him. He was

usually the bad cop, the by-the-book guy. But the kid got to him with that look of fear on his face. "It's nearly midnight. Do you really want her to drag the boy out at this hour? Besides, didn't you do the same thing when Brooke came to town not too long ago? You offered her a place to stay, and look what happened."

"Are you saying you're attracted to Shelby Townsend?"

Cullen blinked. Where did that come from? "What? I met her two minutes before you did."

A cocky grin appeared on Trent's face. "That's all it took for me when I first saw Brooke."

"Well, I'm not you, soldier boy." He called him by his old nickname. Trent had spent a dozen years in the military before coming back here. "Let's get back to the problem at hand. Do you want to toss a woman and a child out at midnight? Besides, by the looks of her vehicle, she doesn't have much extra money for a motel. Why don't you see if you can get ahold of your last tenant, the Donaldsons, and see if they can check out her story?"

Trent shook his head. "I'll call in the morning. Now I'm going home and climbing back into bed with my beautiful wife." He grinned, and Cullen wanted to slug him. "We'll talk tomorrow."

Cullen pointed to the house. "What about the guests?"

"I'll let you handle the pretty brunette. If they rob us blind, I'll send the sheriff after them." With a laugh his brother walked off to his truck.

Cullen just shook his head. When his father had first married Leslie, he and his twin brother, Austin, had been barely ten. And they hated Leslie's thirteen-year-old son, Trent, on sight. It took a few years, but they all got over it, and with his stepmother's love they'd all become somewhat of a family.

He looked up at the house. Did he trust the woman?

He used to rely on his cop instincts, but these days he wasn't so sure. He walked up the steps, knocked on the door and waited until she answered.

The door finally opened and Miss Townsend motioned him inside. "Please, come in, Sheriff."

He stepped across the threshold and caught a whiff of her fragrance, soft and clean like soap. Damn, if she didn't remind him the past year had been a long and lonely one.

"You and the boy can stay for the night and I'll come by in the morning to see about making other arrangements."

"That's not necessary, Sheriff. Ryan and I are planning to head west."

"Do you have somewhere to go?"

She hesitated, then shook her head. "But I have a laptop and I can look for a job."

"The B&B Café is looking for a part-time cook," he blurted out.

She looked surprised at his volunteering the information.

He shrugged. "I only know that because I was in earlier for supper and Bill told me he and Betty needed to cut down their workload. They also run a catering business on the side. I know cooking for cowboys is different than cooking for a restaurant…"

"I am a chef, Sheriff." She combed back her hair with long fingers. "I graduated from culinary school."

"Then it shouldn't be difficult to find employment." He played with the hat in his hands. "If you do plan to stay and get a job maybe we can help you find a place to stay. There is the cottage out back. It's a lot smaller, but there are two bedrooms."

He saw the interest in her blue eyes.

"I'll just need to talk to Trent." His brother Austin was one of the owners, too, but wouldn't care if he rented the place. "Not sure how the Donaldsons left it, but I'm sure it's livable."

"That's very nice of you," she told him. "I'll have to think about it."

"I understand. I should get back on patrol." He didn't move. Why did he hate leaving her alone? He could sense her fear and couldn't help but wonder what was causing it.

"You and your brother are being very generous for letting us stay the night. I'll make sure we clean up before we leave."

"So you're not staying in town?"

"Only if I get employment."

He nodded. "Okay, if you want to try for that job, the B&B Café is just off Main Street on Aspen."

She hugged her robe together. "Thank you again, Sheriff. I'll think about my options. Of course, Ryan has to be my first consideration. I'll let you know tomorrow." She headed to the door, letting him know that he should leave.

He shouldn't care, but he found he wanted to help. Why? Maybe it was because when he had trouble, there'd been few people who wanted to stand by him. Sometimes, it took a stranger to step up and give a person a hand.

He stopped at the door. "I'm new here, too, just a few weeks as the interim sheriff. Hidden Springs is a nice town." What was he, the chamber of commerce? Then he realized what he said was true. Maybe he should take his own advice and give this place a chance.

Chapter Two

The next morning, Shelby packed their suitcases. No matter what happened today, they weren't going to be staying in the farmhouse.

By ten o'clock, Ryan had been fed his usual bowl of Cheerios and they headed into town. Shelby parked her compact car off Main Street and eyed the storefront building, the B&B Café.

Should she go in and see about the job? She glanced in the backseat and saw Ryan busy with his picture album. He kept looking at his mother's photo. She had no way to explain to the boy about the evil of some people. How they could take another life.

"Look, Ryan, we're going to go inside so I can see about getting a job."

"Mama worked. She worked at my school."

"That's right, sweetie. She was a teacher."

"She was going to teach me, too." He blinked really fast. "Now, she's in heaven with Daddy."

"Yes, she is, and he's going to take care of her forever and ever." Shelby had trouble holding back the tears. "So don't worry about her."

Shelby got out of the car, went to the backseat and helped Ryan out, too. They walked into the café, and she opened the glass door. *Here goes.* She released a breath, hoping to relax a little.

Inside, Shelby looked around and decided she liked the down-home atmosphere. Several gingham-checked-cloth-covered tables were situated on a black-and-white-tiled floor, and black leather padded booths ran along the wall under the windows. There were pictures of the area's skiing and hiking trails, and many just of the beautiful Colorado scenery.

A slight woman about fifty-five came out of the back. She had short gray hair, warm brown eyes and a big smile. "I'm thinking you might be Shelby Townsend." She smiled down at the boy. "You must be Ryan."

Her nephew hid behind her. "Yes, I'm Shelby." So the sheriff had been here.

"Welcome to town, I'm Bess Cummings. My husband, Bill, and I own this restaurant and the catering business next door."

"Nice to meet you, Mrs. Cummings."

"Please, call me Bess."

Shelby nodded. "I'm told that you might possibly be looking for some help in the restaurant."

"Could be. We're overworked, especially when the wedding season begins in a month or so. It's hard to run both sides of our business. Oh, pardon my manners." She motioned to the end booth. "Please, go have a seat. Would you like some coffee?"

"Yes, please."

Bess looked at Ryan. "How about some pancakes with fruit? Some strawberries?"

The child's eyes rounded and he looked at Shelby, and she nodded. "That would be nice."

Bess went into the kitchen and returned with two mugs of coffee and a small glass of milk. "I hope this is okay."

"Yes, thank you, milk is fine."

She got Ryan situated with his photo book. "You picked a good time to come in with the breakfast crowd already gone." The door opened and two customers walked in. "That always happens."

A large gentleman came out of the back as two men sat down at the counter. He filled their coffee mugs, then took their orders. "That's Bill. I'll introduce you later." She looked at her. "I hear you're a chef."

The sheriff again? "Yes, I graduated from culinary school in Louisville, Kentucky." She pulled out her folded résumé from her purse. "Here are some of the places I worked."

Bess read over the paper. "I'm impressed. A sous-chef, huh?"

"I just recently moved in to the position when I left town."

"May I ask why you left the restaurant?"

How much should she say? "My sister and nephew were moving here, and they're my only family so I decided to come with them." She glanced at Ryan and lowered her voice. "My sister passed away unexpectedly. So now I'm Ryan's only family."

Bess's hand touched her heart. "I am so sorry for your loss." She looked at Ryan, showing her sorrow. "If there is anything I can do… Of course there is." She looked over the résumé again. "How would you like to work for Bill and me? We're not fancy, and we can't offer you full time yet, but I am curious to see your ideas for our catering business. Our May and June is nearly booked with weddings, so maybe you can add some new items for our menu."

"Really? You want me to help with catering?"

She nodded. "That's when Bill and I really get overwhelmed, and we're too old to run around like that. So if you don't mind working at the restaurant and cooking hamburgers in between a few specialties…"

Wow, she was being offered a job. Did she dare take it? "Of course not. I mean, I can cook a hamburger."

Bess smiled. "Good, because your help would be wonderful, especially with your skill level. I doubt we can pay you what you're worth, but there are good tips working here, and especially in the catering. So if you can deal with that, you're hired."

"Sounds fine to me. Thank you, I'll take the job."

Bess grinned, then turned to her husband. "Bill, get over here and meet our new waitress."

NEARLY TWO HOURS LATER, Shelby drove back to the ranch, excited she had accepted the job. A good one and she had to take it. Step one was taken care of with her getting the job. Now her biggest concern was Ryan. He'd had enough changes in his life already, so she couldn't just drop him off for a stranger to watch him.

Georgia had been adamant about her son's special care. She was an overprotective mother, but with good reason. Ryan had lost his father, Lieutenant Joshua Hughes, while he'd been deployed in Afghanistan three years ago. Ryan never really knew him. Now his mother was gone, too.

Since Georgia's murder, Shelby didn't know whom to trust. Her thoughts turned to Sheriff Brannigan. The law was supposed to help you, but she'd learned that wasn't always the case.

She pulled into the driveway and saw the sheriff's car along with the familiar oversize black truck parked around the side of the house.

"Aunt Shellie, who's here?" Ryan said, with fear in his voice.

"It's okay, Ryan. Looks like Sheriff Brannigan and Mr. Landry."

So the family was here to make sure she was moved out. What was she going to do now? She needed to figure out a place to stay. Maybe a small apartment, but her money was limited until she got her first paycheck. It would take everything she had to get together the first and last months' rent, and she wasn't sure if this job would work out here. Maybe she could find something that she could pay week to week. The savings Shelby had planned on, a lot had been spent on Georgia's burial. So this job was all Shelby had.

She climbed out of the car, helped Ryan from his safety seat in back, then they walked the single step of the guesthouse porch. The door was open, and voices reached her before she saw anyone.

She hated to interrupt. "Hello, is anyone here?" she called out.

Soon a tall blonde woman appeared. "Hi, you must be Shelby." Her green eyes sparkled when she smiled. "I'm Brooke, Trent's wife." She looked at Ryan. "And you're Ryan. My niece, Addy, is about your age."

The boy looked at his aunt and then smiled at the woman.

Shelby held out her hand and shook hers. "It's nice to meet you, Brooke. I apologize for invading your house last night."

"Not your fault." Brooke waved her arm. "Trent talked with Jake Donaldson this morning, and he feels terrible about the mix-up. I hope the guys didn't frighten you too much."

After her dealings with Gil and his police buddies, the

sheriff and Trent Landry were sweethearts. "No, they were very considerate about the situation."

"Well, please come inside. The Donaldsons were great tenants, but still the house needs a good cleaning."

"Wait. Are you saying you want to rent this place to me?"

Brooke paused. "That all depends. If you're staying in Hidden Springs, and did you get the job at the café?"

She hesitated, then nodded to both.

"Then with your employment, I'm sure Trent and Cullen won't have a problem renting to you." Brooke gasped. "Of course, you want to see it first before you commit."

Shelby looked around the small, but cozy, living area. There was a leather sofa, and a high-back chair with two end tables and lamps. An area rug covered the scarred hardwood floors. She was drawn to the brick fireplace, then followed Brooke down the hall to a retro bathroom with green and black tiles. The next stop was a small bedroom with a single bed and dresser.

"This could work for Ryan," she suggested.

Brooke agreed. "Yes, he doesn't need much room." She looked at the boy. "Do you like it, Ryan?"

Her nephew nodded.

They went to the last bedroom, which was a little bigger and held a bare queen-size bed and a dresser. The windows were void of any curtains, but there were shades for privacy.

"If you add your own touches, it would really dress up the place."

She would love to. Question was, could she afford this house? "It's lovely, but I need to know what the rent is."

"I guess we should ask the brothers that question." Brooke smiled. "I love saying that they're brothers. Trent and Cullen hadn't been together in a long time. It's time they were family again."

WHEN CULLEN'S SHIFT ended he hadn't been crazy about going back to his temporary residence at the motel. Instead, he'd stopped for breakfast and somehow he ended up talking with the Cummingses about Shelby Townsend, then called Trent and asked him about renting the guesthouse.

Trent told him it wasn't a problem, but then Cullen would have to live in the main house. He wasn't crazy about that, but it was temporary, like his job.

Damn. Why was he so gung ho on helping this woman?

Two years ago, he wouldn't have lifted a finger to help. So many things had changed, and his life would never be the same. To be on the safe side, he'd run Shelby Townsend's name through the system and found she'd checked out. She was who she said she was. Not even a parking ticket.

Now he was here, cleaning. And if Shelby and Ryan moved in here, they were going to be neighbors.

"So Miss Townsend intrigues you," Trent said as he paused from cleaning the upper cabinet.

"She doesn't have anywhere to go," he said. "It was Hank Donaldson who brought her here for a job. A job that doesn't exist anymore." He continued to toss out all the packaged food and spices in the cupboard that had been left behind. "We've never had a problem about knowing where we'd live." He couldn't imagine having to do it with a child.

"No. Uncle Sam took care of me for over a dozen years. And then Dad left me the Lucky Bar L." Trent gave him a big smile. "And I finally found my home."

Cullen had to admit he was a little envious of his stepbrother. "And that pretty wife of yours."

"I think I heard my name." A smiling Brooke walked

into the kitchen, followed by Shelby and Ryan. He felt a sudden awareness as the woman glanced in his direction.

Trent was the first to speak. "Hey, there, Ryan."

The boy's eyes widened, but he stayed glued to his aunt's side.

Cullen's attention stayed on the pretty aunt. Today she was dressed in a pair of dark slacks and a pretty pink blouse with a long tan coat sweater.

"Hello, Shelby," he finally greeted her.

"Hello, Sheriff," she returned.

"I'm off duty, so call me Cullen."

Trent chuckled. "Heck, he's only been sheriff what, ten days? Call him Cullen all the time."

That got a smile from her, and he wished he'd been the reason for it. "How about Sheriff Cullen?" she joked, and even Ryan laughed.

Cullen looked at the boy. "So you like that, huh, buddy?"

He was rewarded with a bigger grin and a nod. Why did that make his day?

He looked at Shelby. "Did you go to the café?"

She nodded. "Thank you for recommending me for the job."

Trent shot him a look, but he ignored it. "I only told Bess that you might be in today."

"Well, she hired me part-time for the restaurant now, then more hours for the catering side. They have several weddings booked starting next month."

Cullen nodded. "That's good."

She didn't look as happy. "I'm worried about Ryan. We're in a new area and I need someone reliable to watch him. When we planned to work the roundups, he would stay with us."

Brooke spoke up. "I have a few names we use for our son, Chris. There's also St. Francis's preschool. My niece went there last year. I'll get my phone and give you all the info. So does that help you make the decision about staying?"

Shelby nodded, but she was pretty sure she couldn't afford to live here. "I guess that depends on the rent for the cottage."

Trent looked at Cullen, then his brother said, "Why don't we go a hundred a week until you see if everything works out with the job?"

Her eyes grew wide. "Oh, no. I can't accept that. That's...too generous."

Trent raised a hand. "This was our mother's ranch." His voice grew husky. "I have no doubt she'd offer you the same arrangement. Sometimes we all need some help to get started."

Brooke stepped in, and slipped her arm around her husband's waist, then said, "How about we give you a trial period, then increase the rent then?" She looked at Cullen. "Do you both agree to that? A trial period then if Shelby wants to stay you'll raise the rent."

Cullen looked at the pretty brunette, suddenly hoping she'd take the agreement and stay around.

THAT AFTERNOON, SHELBY had their meager belongings moved over to the cottage. With the brothers giving her a cut in rent, she agreed to take the place only if she'd be the one to finish cleaning it.

She looked around and saw the beauty of the place. Okay, it was small, but the brick fireplace and the hardwood floors, scarred or not, gave it character. She'd mostly lived in apartments, with roommates, but after finishing culinary school, she'd hoped to finally put down some roots. Could Hidden Springs be that place?

She could see the brothers both wanted to help her, but

she didn't want to be beholden to anyone. Most of her life, she and her older sister had been in the foster care system. A lot of those years she'd lost touch with Georgia. They'd found each other only about a year ago when she'd learned about the hell her sister had been going through with Gil Bryant. Shelby had seen firsthand what Georgia's ex-boyfriend could do when angered. She'd shown up one day and found Georgia beaten and bruised, but her sister refused to go to the ER.

Since Gil was a cop in the small Southern town, his fellow officers protected their brother. Even after Georgia broke up with him, he still got away with coming into her apartment and terrorizing her. He swore that she could never leave him.

Not having the option to call for any protection, Georgia had no choice but to take her son and disappear, and Shelby was going with them. They'd planned to leave Kentucky and come to Colorado to work on a ranch.

Then came the day they were to leave town. At five o'clock, Shelby had her car packed with all their possessions. She picked Ryan up at preschool, then drove to the designated meeting spot at the strip mall. When nightfall came and Georgia hadn't shown up, Shelby got worried, and knew in her gut something had gone wrong.

After dropping Ryan off at the babysitter, she drove to the house, but a block away she saw the police car and flashing lights, then the coroner's vans. Panic took over and she jumped out of the car and ran to the house, but it was too late. Gil had gotten to Georgia. He'd killed her. There wasn't any proof that he'd been the one who shot her. Of course he had an alibi. Several of his fellow officers backed him up.

She'd never trust a cop again.

She swiped at a tear. That was when she heard her

name. She swung around to find Cullen Brannigan. He was dressed in a pair of jeans and a henley shirt. She couldn't help but look over the expansive chest, then realizing what she was doing, she looked at his somber face.

"Oh, Cullen." She went to the opened door. "Is something wrong?"

He shook his head, but held out the two big bags in his hand. "Brooke sent me over with some cleaning supplies. She was at the store and realized there weren't any left here."

She started to take the bags, but he shook his head. So she motioned him inside and led him into the kitchen. He followed her into the room lined with older white cabinets and butcher-block counters. The floor was worn but went with the rest of the house. She had boxes of pots and pans and her seasoning and spices on the table. And her extravagance had been her specialty knives.

"Thank you. This will help a lot. Once I get the kitchen organized and unpack my things, I was planning to go pick up some food, too." She was excited that she would have an adequate kitchen to work in.

Their eyes connected, and there was a tightening in her chest that quickly spread through her body. She glanced away.

"I believe there's shelf paper in there, so you can put away all your things."

"It's crazy, but the kitchen is important to me."

He nodded. "Well, I'd hold off awhile on making too much food," he suggested. "I have a feeling Brooke and Laurel will be bringing some food dishes by later."

"Oh, they don't need to do that."

Cullen crossed his arms over his massive chest. "Sorry, there's no stopping them. You may be a professional chef, but you'll be getting some pretty tasty food."

He leaned forward. "Laurel's mother is quite the baker, too. Her oatmeal cookies are out of this world."

She nodded. "Sounds like you've sampled a few."

"Of course. Luckily, since I've been here I've managed to work off the extra pounds by lifting hay bales for Trent."

"So you don't do any ranching like your brother?"

He shook his head. "I lived in Denver until this job came up. I really haven't thought much about what to do with my share of this land. Trent likes that I'm here, and will probably talk me into getting some animals." He looked out the window that faced the big empty barn. "I wouldn't mind getting a horse or two." He wasn't sure right now. "I want to concentrate on my job and settle in." He knew that since he was part owner of this property, Trent would encourage him to stay permanently.

Before she could ask, he said, "Trent's mother was married to my father. She died suddenly last month."

Shelby caught the sadness in his voice. "I'm sorry. She must have really loved you boys to leave you all this."

He nodded. "It's one of the reasons I took the interim sheriff job. Sheriff Ted Carson had a heart attack."

"Oh, I hope he's okay."

"From what I hear, he's doing fine, but he has to recover from his surgery."

"So what are you planning to do after that?"

He shook his head. "Seems we're in the same predicament, Shelby Townsend. I'm not sure what's going to happen in the future."

Chapter Three

The next evening after the sun had gone down, Cullen stood at his kitchen window looking toward the cottage. After Trent's strong urging, he'd officially moved in to the ranch house. Now his attention was focused on the other tenants living about a hundred yards away from his back door. Bright lights illuminated the small structure, and with the lack of curtains, he could easily see inside.

Shelby Townsend was busy at the stove, maybe cooking one of her specialties. Her rich mahogany hair was pulled up into a big clip, but some wild curls found their way out. She had on an oversize T-shirt and a pair of jeans covering her trim figure.

He quickly shook away his wayward thoughts and turned his attention to the table, where the boy sat, going through his photo book. Shelby said something to the child that caused them both to laugh. A soft lyrical sound seemed to vibrate through his chest, causing that familiar ache, reminding him of his solitary life.

He turned away, knowing that Miss Townsend could be a distraction if he let her. He thought back to when his shift had ended this morning, and how he had to fight from stopping by the café. Even after one of the deputies came into work all chatty about the pretty brunette Bess had hired, he'd driven home. Well, back to the motel, but just long enough to pack up his things and finally move in to the ranch house. He didn't want the new tenants to be out here all alone.

Something else nagged at him, causing him to want to know more about the attractive, blue-eyed woman who'd moved twelve hundred miles from her home for a temporary job. The cop in him was suspicious of her motives, especially after the recent death of her sister. So many questions.

The microwave buzzer went off, pulling him back to reality. He realized he'd been standing there in the dark looking into other people's lives.

Hell, he was one pathetic guy who didn't have a life. He turned away and took the casserole out of the microwave. Once the word of his move had circulated through the Hidden Springs family, the contributions poured in, starting with sheets and towels. Mysteriously, his refrigerator had been stocked with food staples; butter, eggs, bacon and milk. Brooke had added a chicken casserole, and she'd also taken some to Shelby and Ryan at the cottage.

Cullen walked over and flipped on the overhead light, then reached in the drawer and found a fork, then poured a glass of milk and sat down at the large table.

He wasn't sure if he was ready to make a home here in this small town, not beyond the next few months of his interim job anyway. He wasn't the down-home type of guy.

Ever since he'd been a little boy, he wanted to be a cop like his dad. He'd idolized Neal Brannigan, the highly decorated, by-the-book cop.

And it had been Cullen's goal to follow after him.

Since the day he'd entered the police academy, he'd been dedicated to his job, a job that he had learned would cost him relationships and friends.

He'd worked his way up the ranks from patrol officer and earned detective, then went into a special department for white-collar crimes. He found he liked it, and best of all, he was good at going after cybercriminals. Then he messed with the wrong people, and he got too close to breaking up an illegal credit card ring.

The next thing he knew he'd been arrested for taking bribes. They found large deposits in his bank account, all the evidence he'd compiled on the ring had disappeared and Internal Affairs came in to investigate. He'd been humiliated, but the worst part, he didn't get any support from his own father. Captain Neal Brannigan said he had to stay neutral. Cullen knew his father had always been a hard-ass, but he never thought the man would desert his own son.

It had taken nearly a year, and a chunk of his savings, before he was cleared of all the charges, and reinstated in the department. The question was, did he want to go back? How could he trust his fellow officers, if they didn't have his back? Maybe that was the reason he didn't trust many people.

Cullen took a last bite of food, then carried his plate to the sink, his thoughts still on his new neighbor. Even though he found nothing about Shelby Townsend, he also searched the national database for information on her sister, Georgia Hughes. Only a month ago Mrs. Hughes was murdered in her home.

He glanced at the cottage again. It seemed that Miss Townsend had withheld a lot of information the other night. Not that she'd been involved in any criminal activities, but the cop in him sure was curious.

There was a soft knock on the back door and he wondered if it could be Trent. He walked through the kitchen and flipped on the light in the mudroom to find Shelby and Ryan standing on the stoop.

He opened the door, but before he could speak, Shelby spoke, "Good evening, Sheriff."

"Hello, Shelby. Ryan."

"I don't want to bother you. I only wanted to drop these off to say thank you for all your help."

"Not a problem." He took the covered plate. "What is this?"

"Cookies," Ryan announced.

Cullen couldn't help but smile. "Please come inside for a moment."

Shelby shook her head. "We really can't. I should get Ryan to bed."

He found he didn't want her to leave. "At least come in and tell me how work went today." He was hoping to get more information about her sister. And he had four long hours of solitude before he left for his shift on patrol. "Or are you afraid I won't like your cookies?"

She straightened. "Please, Sheriff. If there's one thing I'm sure of, it's my baking skills."

So he hit a sore spot. "Just for some coffee, and some milk for Ryan and share a cookie."

"Okay, but not too long. I have the early shift tomorrow."

"And I have the late shift tonight." He allowed them in ahead of him. He inhaled her soft womanly scent. Whoa, she was intoxicating.

In the kitchen, he watched as Shelby looked around.

"The place is pretty big, isn't it?" he said.

"Yes, it is. I didn't get a chance to see everything when we arrived. I love all the character." She ran her hand over the tiled counters. The cabinets had been painted white, and the floors were the same hardwood that ran throughout the house. She went to the older stove.

"Lucky you. This is an O'Keefe & Merritt stove." She ran her hand reverently over the chrome handles and white porcelain top. "I know the newer models are more efficient, but I love this. Reminds me of the one at my grandmother Ivy's house."

Good opening for some info. "Does she still live there…in Kentucky?"

She shook her head. "There isn't anyone else left, just Ryan and me."

He caught the sadness in her eyes. "I'm sorry. Please, have a seat," he said, but Ryan had wandered through the dining room to the living area. He stood staring at the big screen over the fireplace. The only thing Cullen had gotten done since yesterday had been to mount his television.

"Hey, Ryan, would you like to watch a movie?"

The boy looked at his aunt and said, "*Thomas the Tank Engine*, please."

"You just said the magic words. We don't have a television right now." She looked at her nephew. "Maybe next time, sweetie. We can't stay long tonight, remember?" The child didn't argue. He just climbed up on the chair at the table.

Cullen walked to the coffeemaker, took down two mugs from above and poured them both a cup. "Cream or sugar?" he asked. "Whoa, I'm not sure if I have any sugar. I do have milk, though."

"Black is fine," she said.

"How did your first day at the café go?"

She smiled. "Good. Bill and Bess are sweethearts to work for. Bess even let Ryan stay at the restaurant. She made a place in a corner of the kitchen away from the work areas. A little table where he could color and play on his tablet." She shrugged. "It's temporary. I'm looking into some day care, but this week he can stay with me."

"That's great." Cullen brought the full mugs to the table as she removed the foil from the plate of cookies. Oatmeal. He got a glass and filled it half-full with milk for Ryan and set it down in front of him. He took the chair across from the pair.

Shelby felt nervous being here with Cullen. She was attracted to this man, and that wasn't something she needed to be thinking about, or giving him any ideas about being available. There was no time, or room, in her life for a man. Too bad.

She took a sip of the rich brew with a touch of almond favor. "This is good. The only problem might be I'm up all night."

Cullen nodded. "And I need it to stay awake for my shift."

"Why is the sheriff working the night shift? Aren't you the boss?"

"The *interim* sheriff, and I'm the new guy here. I'm trying to get to know the area." He took a drink of his coffee. "I should be used to pulling an all-nighter, but my body tells me differently."

She couldn't help but watch the man. Just his good looks drew her, but it was more. He had a way of making her aware of herself as a woman, maybe too aware. Working in a male-dominated field, she had to become one of the guys to survive in her profession.

His gaze met hers. The hazel color was almost green... his mouth was tempting. He didn't make her feel like one of the guys.

She glanced down at the plate. "You haven't tried my cookies." She handed one to Ryan.

Never taking his eyes off her, Cullen reached for one and took a bite. She watched him chew, waiting for his praise. It didn't take long.

An approving rumble erupted from deep in his chest, then he smiled. "You weren't lying, Miss Townsend. This is great. What's your secret?"

She shook her head. "I can't divulge that. Maybe one day I'll want to open my own shop and become a millionaire."

"The million-dollar cookie. Has a nice ring to it." He quickly finished one, then reached for another. "Are you going to take over the baking for Bess?"

She shrugged. "I'm not sure. I made a sampler plate of things to take into work tomorrow."

"A sampler plate? Why did I only get to test oatmeal?"

She hid a smile. "Because that was the one kind you talked about."

"So if I put in my order now, will you bring me, say, chocolate chip, maybe sugar, or peanut butter?"

Was he flirting with her? Darn, it had been so long she couldn't even tell. "We'll see."

He leaned back in the chair, crossing his arms over his chest.

"I'm glad you brought these by tonight. I wanted to stop at the cottage to see if you're doing okay, but didn't want you to feel I was checking up on you and Ryan."

Tempting as this man was, she had to ignore the little flutters of excitement. "Thank you for allowing us the privacy."

"I want you to know that you're safe here."

She nodded, feeling her breath locked in her lungs as she recalled the terror of the past few weeks. Would she ever feel safe again? "Why wouldn't I be safe out here?"

"You were all alone on a ranch, but I'm here now."

That still didn't help with her trust issues. Cullen Brannigan made her nervous, not in a fearful way, but in a way that could be just as dangerous.

ABOUT ELEVEN THIRTY, Cullen was dressed for work. He took his sidearm out of the lockbox he'd decided to keep on the high shelf in the hall closet. He slipped the Glock into his holster, snapped the leather strap over it and adjusted his utility belt. He wore a pair of dark blue trousers, and his light blue uniform shirt with his sheriff's badge pinned over the pocket. As a detective, he carried only cuffs and his sidearm. He wasn't used to all this bulk. Since he'd be inside the station tonight, he didn't put on his Kevlar vest.

He grabbed his travel mug filled with coffee for his twenty-minute drive into town. He reached for his gray cowboy hat off the hook, then he turned the lock before closing the back door. He started for his patrol car when he heard the child's scream.

What the hell? He froze in alert, then glanced at the cottage to see the place was dark, except for the porch light. He listened and then heard another frantic cry. That had to be Ryan.

He set his coffee on the hood of the car and hurried toward the cottage, but he passed the porch and went around the side to Ryan's bedroom. He found the window untouched. No sign of any break-in.

Then he heard Shelby's voice. "It's okay, Ryan. I'm here, and no one will hurt you."

Cullen glanced in the window and saw her seated on the bed, holding the child. He moved away, but listened, telling himself it was to make sure they were both okay.

"He hurt Mommy. He's gonna get us," the child cried. "I want my mommy."

Shelby hugged Ryan as tight as she could, but even her secure hold didn't stop the child's trembling. She cursed Gil Bryant. He might never have put a hand on Ryan, but he had to watch as the bastard hit his mother.

"I know you do, sweetheart, but we talked about this. Your mother is in heaven. She's safe with your dad."

"I want to go, too."

"Oh, Ryan." She blinked back tears. "I would miss you so much."

Suddenly a loud knock sounded on the front door. Ryan gasped.

"Shelby. It's Cullen. Are you okay?"

She sighed in relief. "It's Cullen." She lifted the boy from the bed. "We better go answer the door." She carried the child with her, knowing she couldn't leave him alone in the bedroom.

She checked through the peephole to see the man dressed in uniform. "Oh, boy." She opened the door to the sheriff. He removed his hat as he stepped inside.

"Is everything all right?"

With her nod, he turned his attention to Ryan. "I heard you scream, son. Did you have a bad dream?"

Shelby was surprised when Ryan nodded against her shoulder. "Sorry he disturbed you," she said.

Cullen put on a smile. "He didn't, I was headed into work. Since there's no one around for miles, I wanted to make sure everyone here was all right."

His empathy drew her. "Thank you, Sheriff."

He nodded, then glanced back at the boy. "Hey, Ryan, did you know that part of my job is to check under beds and in closets? If you want, I can check yours."

Ryan raised his head, looked at her, then nodded.

"Okay, I'll go and make sure it's all clear." He winked at Shelby, then took off down the hall to the first bedroom. The light went on, then a few seconds later, she heard, "The closet is clear." A few more seconds, "Under the bed is clear, too."

Sheriff Brannigan walked out and toward them. "I

checked everything, including shutting and locking the windows. It's safe to go back to sleep."

Shelby looked at Ryan. "I think it's time you go back to bed, okay?"

The boy nodded and Shelby carried him down the hall and into the bedroom. She handed her nephew the iPad and let him look at a movie. She probably shouldn't spoil him, but they both needed some sleep.

She kissed him on his head, then walked out but didn't close the door. She came back into the living room and joined Cullen. "Thank you, Sheriff. What you did was very nice."

He shook his head. "I'm glad I could help, and I thought you were going to call me Cullen."

She glanced over him decked out in his uniform. "Dressed like that, it's hard not to call you Sheriff." Surprisingly, the uniform hadn't scared Ryan.

"I'm still getting used to the title and the uniform."

He studied her for a moment.

She was suddenly aware of her thin pajamas. She crossed her arms over her chest, but didn't hide much. That was the least of her troubles. She had more important things to hide from this man.

"Does Ryan have a lot of nightmares?"

She shrugged. "It's a new place. He has trouble with change. That's an issue with kids on the…spectrum." She wasn't about to go into Ryan's medical disorder at this time. "We're dealing."

"Since I'm your only neighbor, is there anything I should know about his…condition?"

"Since he's usually with me, I don't believe so. He's just recently lost his mother, and he's dealing with a lot for a little boy."

"That's got to be rough on him and on you." He looked

at her another moment, then checked his watch. "I need to get to work." He took a card out of his pocket, along with a pen, then jotted something down. "Here is the number of the sheriff's office, and also there's my cell number."

"I don't need to call you. Ryan just had a bad dream."

"Whatever you call it, I'm here and I'll do whatever it takes to keep you both safe." He turned and walked out, leaving her wanting to run after him and take what he was offering her.

"Thank you, Cullen," she whispered into the darkness. If only she could trust him enough to share her secrets. But the stakes were too high.

Chapter Four

The next morning the sun was shining bright when Cullen walked out of his office at the station. He greeted the day shift, deputies Tory Michaels, Brad Rogers and Sheila Brown.

"If you need me, call. For anything," he told his second in command, Lieutenant Rogers, then he walked by the dispatcher, Connie Lara, at her workstation.

The midfifties woman truly ran the place, and he appreciated her efficiency. He was sure Ted Carson was resting easy knowing his sister was keeping an eye open.

"Have a good day, Sheriff," she called.

"You, too, Connie. I'm going home to sleep." He walked through the glass doors and got into his truck, but instead of heading to the ranch, he drove across Main Street and parked in front of the B&B Café.

"So shoot me, I'm hungry," he murmured as he got out and went inside the cozy diner. He glanced around the place crowded with customers. It was after eight o'clock. He guessed these people didn't have to work for a living. There was a lone vacant spot at the counter, and he grabbed it. Bill Cummings walked by with an empty mug, set it on the counter and filled it.

"Thanks, Bill. Are you running a special this morning?" he asked.

The café owner nodded. "You bet. It's Shelby's French toast, her eggs Benedict, and her biscuits and gravy." He reached for a basket. "Here, try one of her apple spice muffins. You don't even need butter."

Cullen grabbed one. It was still warm. He took a bite, and his taste buds went crazy.

The sixty-something café owner leaned against the counter. "Bess and I haven't even started tapping into her other talents."

"Well, it looks like she's caused a boom in your business."

Bill grinned. "Yeah, and I might have to hire another waitress."

"I'll have the French toast and a side of bacon with scrambled eggs."

"Got it, Sheriff."

Over the next ten minutes he drank his one cup of coffee, then switched to orange juice so he could sleep when he got home. Finally his platter of food arrived just as Shelby walked out of the kitchen with little Ryan in tow.

She was dressed in a white cook's smock and her hair was pulled back into a ponytail, making her blue eyes look even bigger. Her face was clean of makeup with just a little lip gloss on her mouth. Even with his lack of sleep, he felt the jolt of awareness.

She walked around to his side of the counter. The café was clearing out. "Morning, Sheriff."

"Morning to you, too. Hi, Ryan."

The boy smiled.

"Join me?" He reached down and lifted Ryan to the vacant stool beside him. The child was carrying his prize picture book.

"Hi, Sheriff Cullen."

That made Cullen grin. "So, no more monsters?"

The blond-haired boy shook his head. "All gone."

"Good. I'll chase them away any time you want. Okay?"

The boy nodded. "Okay."

Shelby sat beside her nephew. "So how was your breakfast?"

"You know how it was. Delicious. Another secret recipe?"

She nodded. "My grandmother's. She taught me more than any culinary school."

He watched the sadness play over her pretty features. He wanted to reach out and comfort her.

"I bet she'd be proud that you learned your craft so well."

Shelby looked at him. "I hope so. She was the best part of my childhood. She took me in when no one…" Shelby stopped and glanced at the busy kitchen. "I need to get back to work."

She started to help Ryan down, but the boy resisted. "Want to stay with the sheriff."

Shelby opened her mouth, but Cullen stepped in. "He can sit here awhile until I finish."

She didn't look too certain. "Trust me, Shelby."

She nodded then walked back to the kitchen, leaving him wondering what in her life caused her to be so distrusting. He took a sip of coffee. That was something he hoped he could change.

LATER THAT AFTERNOON, Cullen finally got up from bed, showered and dressed to go downstairs. He looked at the living room. Sheets still covered the furniture, except for the sofa, where he could sit and watch television. Maybe it was time he got his things from storage. He combed his fingers through his short hair, thinking he needed coffee before he made any decisions about his future. He turned and walked through the dining room to the kitchen.

Once the coffee had been made and he took his first sip, he began to slowly feel human again. That was when he heard the sound of an approaching vehicle. He looked out the window to see Trent's truck pulling a trailer and parking beside the barn.

"What the hell?"

He put down his mug and headed outside just as his stepbrother climbed out of the cab. "Good afternoon, Sheriff."

Cullen nodded. "That depends on what's inside the trailer."

Trent put on a big smile. "Just a couple of old guys who need a place to retire. Well, one is a lady." He walked to the back of the trailer, unpinned the gate and lowered it. Inside there were two horses.

"Whoa. Are they staying here?"

Trent paused and slipped his hands into his pockets. "Yeah, if you don't have a problem. I don't have any extra stalls at my place, and since this barn is empty, I thought I could board them here."

Before Cullen could even figure out what was going on, Trent was slowly backing a golden-brown bay gelding down the ramp. At one time the horse must have been a beauty, and the good bloodlines showed in the equine.

Trent held on to the lead rope. "This is Dakota Dancer." He gave the reins to Cullen and went to get the other horse, a little black mare, with white stocks and a star blaze on her forehead. "This is Sassy Girl."

"So how long are they going to be staying here?"

"Not sure." They walked toward the corral, opened the gate and released the horses.

"I know. I know. They're older horses, but they're

still perfectly healthy. I mean, I wouldn't suggest you take them on a hard ride, but I can't allow them to be put down."

Cullen didn't like that idea, either. "So you're opening a horse rescue here?"

Trent's eyes lit up. "Hey, not a bad idea."

Cullen didn't like where this was heading. "And who's going to be feeding these two and mucking out their stalls? From what I remember from childhood, when you feed animals, something comes out the other end that needs to be cleaned up."

Trent laughed. "Well, I thought you could handle the feedings. Maybe I can hire a high school kid to keep the barn and stalls clean, or I can send one of my hands over."

Cullen stood on the bottom railing and watched the two horses run around the corral. Although he couldn't see any evidence, he had to ask, "Have these two been abused?"

Trent shook his head. "Not beaten, but likely neglected. Okay, they were abandoned and left on their own." He sighed. "The animal rescue couldn't take them, and because of their age, they'd probably be put down."

The black mare came over and nudged at Trent's hand, looking for attention. He couldn't resist and petted her. She blew out a loud breath and bobbed her head. She was a sweetheart. Not to be left out, Dakota came over and wanted his turn.

"See what I mean?" Trent said. "We have room here, and the means for some feed."

Cullen tried not to get attached, but these two made it difficult. "What happens when I leave here?"

Trent shrugged. "Let's not worry about that now. We can set up a schedule for everyone to help out. I just need some stalls to protect them from the weather." He turned to his brother. "So what do you think? Will you help out?"

"Hey, this was your mother's place."

Trent frowned. "She wanted you and Austin to have a part of this place, too."

Leslie might have been his stepmother, but to Cullen she was a true mother. His biological mother had died when he and Austin were only ten. Leslie had worked tirelessly to make them a family again when she married their father and brought the brooding thirteen-year-old Trent into the household. It wasn't instant love between the boys.

Cullen tried to hide his smile at the memories. "Okay, it's not a bad idea. So could I ride Dancer?"

"You could, but if you want a good hard ride, I'll bring over one of my saddle horses."

He found he was excited about the idea. "We'll see."

A familiar compact pulled into the driveway. Shelby and Ryan were home. Cullen felt a little kick start around his heart. He was anxious to see how the boy would be around horses.

Once they were out of the car, he motioned for them to come over. Shelby took Ryan's hand, and they started toward him. He couldn't seem to take his eyes off her sexy walk in those formfitting jeans.

She reached them, and she looked first at Trent. "Hi, Trent." Then she turned to him and smiled, and his gut tightened. "Hi, Sheriff."

"Hello, you two." He leaned down to the child. "Want to see who moved in today?"

The boy nodded and reached up so Cullen could lift him. He hoisted the boy up and put him on the railing of the wooden fence. He called to the horses, and soon they came to the railing. So they'd been trained well.

Cullen reached out his hand and stroked the horses.

"This is Dakota and this is Sassy. They'd like you to pet them."

The boy looked at Shelby to see her nod also. "Go ahead, Ryan."

Cullen was a little surprised that Shelby wasn't more protective. Then he got a bigger surprise when she came to the railing and greeted the horses herself.

"Here, like this, Ryan." She rubbed her hand over Dancer's face, and the gelding loved it. "He's gentle," she said. "Now, you rub Sassy." She took the boy's hand and ran it over the horse's face.

Ryan giggled. "Tickles."

"It's a good tickle," Shelby said.

With Ryan busy with the horses, she asked Cullen, "You're boarding horses now?"

He nodded to his brother. "It's more like Trent rescued them." He shrugged, admitting he wasn't the hero in this story. "And we have room here in the barn."

She smiled, and Cullen felt the impact deep in his gut.

"Good job, Sheriff," she said. "Come on, Ryan, I need to fix us some dinner." She said goodbye to Trent, then started off toward the cottage, but stopped and looked back. "Sheriff, it's only leftovers, but there's plenty if you'd like to come by about six."

Without waiting for an answer, she walked off.

"Whoa," Trent said and slapped Cullen on the back. "Nice invitation, bro. You gonna go?"

"I shouldn't." Yet, he couldn't take his eyes off her cute rear end. "I can't get involved." There were too many unanswered questions about Shelby Townsend.

Trent nodded. "I went through the same thing about two years ago with Brooke. Some of us just don't trust easily. But hey, you'd be a fool not to take a second look at her."

He thought back to the past year of his life. "It won't be the first time I've been called that."

AN HOUR LATER, Shelby was calling herself every kind of crazy. What had she been thinking? She had no business asking the sheriff to dinner. Her time here was temporary. She might need to move on just to keep Ryan safe. He was her first and only concern. She was the child's only family, and Georgia trusted her to be his guardian.

The picture of her sweet new employers, Bess and Bill Cummings, came to mind. She knew she'd impressed them with her skills at the restaurant. She loved that the diner was filled up most of the day with customers wanting to eat her food. And she couldn't wait to do her first wedding reception. A couple had a tasting in a few weeks, and Shelby wanted to come up with something special. If the truth be told, she didn't want to leave here.

There was a knock on the door, and her heart skipped a beat. She didn't have time to analyze the reaction, and went to answer the door. She stopped in the kitchen doorway to see that Ryan had let Cullen in.

The sheriff had crouched down to her nephew's size. "Hey, buddy. It might be a good idea if you ask who is there before you open the door."

The boy's blue eyes widened with fear. "Because of monsters?"

"Just because there might be a stranger."

The boy nodded. "Okay."

"Good." Cullen stood and looked across the room to Shelby. "Hi. I hope I'm not too early."

"No, I'm just heating up the lasagna in the oven."

He inhaled a long breath, causing his already-developed chest to expand more. "I thought I smelled something garlicky."

"Probably the bread." She motioned for him to follow her. "Come into the kitchen. I'm finishing up the salad."

"Need help?" he asked.

Need help with what? He sure didn't need any more help being sexy, or too handsome for his own good, or for being too nice to Ryan. He was guilty to all the above. She needed to keep her radar sharp, because this man made her forget all her instincts. Not good.

"I think everything's just about ready."

He stepped up to the small table. "Wow, this all looks pretty good for leftovers." He looked down at the red-checkered tablecloth, and white plates set out with a wooden bowl filled with salad greens. Candles. Had she overdone it?

"I should have brought some wine."

She shook her head. "Don't you have to work tonight?"

"No, I'm off tonight. Of course, I'm on call. So you're probably right, I shouldn't drink. I don't like to have any alcohol if I'm going to get behind the wheel."

Not every law enforcement officer felt that way. She recalled seeing Gil drunk when he showed up at Georgia's door. She shook away the bad memory.

"I'm glad. There are too many crazies out there already."

He nodded in agreement. "Well, I'm hoping I don't have to go any farther than from here to my bed next door."

"Long week?"

"A long two weeks getting acquainted with the area and the way they do things here. These men love Sheriff Carson. I'm an interloper in their community."

"You're only doing your job."

"Law enforcement is a special brotherhood. We take care of each other… Or most of them do."

She knew all about the close connection. She slipped on pot holders and took the pan of lasagna from the oven, then set it on the hot plate on the table. She called for Ryan, then motioned for Cullen to sit down.

After a short blessing, Shelby picked up the plates and began dishing out helpings of the Italian dish. "Are the other deputies not cooperating with you?"

"No, but I'm the temporary new guy. They're ready to tell me when I do something different from the sheriff."

She enjoyed watching him eat so…enthusiastically. "How do you handle that?"

He tore off some bread. "I just let them tell me how things are normally done. Unless it sounds so off-the-wall I'll go along with them, or I go ask Connie Lara, our dispatcher, and the sheriff's sister." He grinned and took a big bite and chewed. "This is great."

"Thank you."

"Another of Grandma's recipes?"

She nodded. "What can I say? She was a good cook."

Ryan picked up his fork, and said, "It's my favorite."

Cullen took another big bite, and groaned while he chewed his food, then said, "I'm thinking it's mine, too."

Ryan giggled.

Cullen winked at her nephew, and something melted around Shelby's heart. She could get into trouble if she wasn't careful. She had to stay alert and not fall into a false sense of security. Gil was out there. She didn't doubt that he had the means to find her. Why? What did he want from her? Well, he wasn't getting any more. He'd already stolen her sister.

Out of the blue, Ryan asked, "Can I ride your horse, Sheriff?"

Shelby started to answer, but Cullen was faster. "I'm not sure. The horses just moved in to their new home.

They might be a little scared right now. So we better wait for a while so we can see how much they like little kids." He looked at Shelby. "And your going riding is a decision your aunt has to make."

They both looked at her. Great, now what should she do? *Oh, Georgia, I wish you were here.*

Chapter Five

After dinner, Shelby helped Ryan bathe and get ready for bed. Once he was tucked in, she kissed him and let him play on the tablet for his allotted twenty minutes. She closed the door, but stood in the hall, thinking about the good-looking man still in her kitchen. While doing dishes earlier he'd discovered a leaky faucet and offered to fix it.

She couldn't just leave him alone in there. She walked back to find the man stretched out on his back under the sink, his Levi's riding low on his narrow hips. He had removed his Western shirt so as not to get it dirty, and so he was working in his undershirt. When he reached up to turn something, the fabric rode up, revealing his flat stomach and a swirl of dark hair.

She closed her eyes, trying not to let this man affect her. It wasn't working.

Suddenly there was a clang, then a chain of curse words. He lifted his head, then she heard the thud and more curse words.

She squatted down next to his prone body. "Cullen, are you okay?"

He slid out from under the sink, and sat up. His face was close to hers. Yet, she couldn't seem to move away.

"Yeah, just bumped my head." He rubbed the sore spot.

"Here, let me see it." She leaned closer and began to

look for blood on his crown. Dear Lord, the man smelled good, a mixture of soap and a hint of aftershave. Had he put on aftershave for her?

"So what's the verdict? Did you find anything?"

"No, it looks okay, but I could get you some ice." She was once again zoned in on his rich hazel eyes.

He finally broke the hold with a shake of his head. "I don't need any ice, just another-size wrench. I'll get it when I come by tomorrow to fix the pipe."

"You don't have to do that."

"As your landlord, I need to have everything in working order."

She sat back on her heels. "Really, I've lived in a lot of places and a lot of things broke, but none of the landlords rushed to fix them."

He didn't hide his smile. Wow, another heart-stopper. She wasn't going to survive this man living next door.

"I guess you've been living in the wrong places."

"You can say that again."

She stood up. She was entirely too close to this dangerous man. She saw that he was interested in her, too. No. Men were out of the question. She had Ryan to think about. So for now, Cullen Brannigan was off-limits.

"Look, what I mean is, just take your time to fix it. It's not so bad that you have to spend your day off doing the repair."

He stood and wiped his hands on a towel. "No, I'll probably be spending it feeding and caring for my new boarders, Sassy and Dakota."

She smiled. "They are beauties. I'd say you are pretty lucky to have them."

"Yeah, it's been a long time since I've had horses around. Do you ride?" he asked.

She nodded. "A long time ago on my grandmother's farm. When she died they sold the place and the stock."

"I take it you were too young to inherit the place."

She glanced away. "Her brother, Harry, got it." He gladly took possession of the property, but no thoughts of taking her grandkids.

"I'm sorry," he said.

She looked up to see the concern on his face. "It's okay, I was only twelve and it was a long time ago."

"Did you spend a lot of time on the farm?"

"Georgia and I lived there with our Nonnie permanently." She glanced away. "Our mother had died in a car accident."

He folded the towel and set it aside. "So you went to live with your dad?"

"No, he couldn't take us." She didn't want to talk about this. "Oh, my, look at the time. I need to go to work early in the morning. I won't be home all day, but you're welcome to come in and fix the faucet. If you really want to."

He looked at her like he wanted to ask more, but nodded. "Sure." He gathered up his tools and headed out of the kitchen. At the front door he stopped and said, "Thank you for dinner. It was delicious." He frowned. "I'm a little disappointed there weren't any oatmeal raisin cookies."

She couldn't stop her grin. "I apologize. I was running late."

Cullen smiled, too. "I'll tell you what. If you bake me some of your famous cookies, I'll let you ride Sassy."

Excitement rushed through her. "You have tack for the horses?"

"Yes. They could use some cleaning, but there're bridles, halters and saddles." He raised a hand. "First, I want to try out the horses to see what their temperaments are."

"From what I saw today, those horses are as gentle as lambs, and happy to have a home. Your brother must be a real softy for rescuing them."

"Don't let him hear you say that. He's ex-military and spent nearly a dozen years in the army."

She smiled. "And now, he has a lovely wife named Brooke and a son, Christopher, who are his whole world."

When she saw his frown, she added, "I'm sorry. Bess talked about your brother and his family." Shelby had also heard about Trent's childhood and how he'd tragically lost his nine-year-old brother.

"Did Bess also tell you how Trent's tragedy gave me and my brother a wonderful mother? And Leslie left me part of this ranch?"

She shook her head, wishing she'd kept her mouth shut. "I'm terribly sorry, Cullen."

He raised a hand to stop her. "It's okay. I just need to get used to living in a small town. Of course, in my experience, the big cities can be just about as bad. Thank you again for supper. Good night." He opened the door and left.

Shelby sat down on the sofa. It seemed that everyone had tragedy in their lives. And her best solution was not to get involved, because she had enough to deal with.

BY THE NEXT AFTERNOON, Cullen had put in a full day of physical labor. After hearing Shelby's car leave that morning, he'd gotten up and showered, then came out to feed his two new boarders. The horses were pretty happy to see him, too. After he filled their grain buckets, he proceeded to check out the barn.

He began with the tack room. He started to organize what was worth saving, and what was beyond repair and he could toss out.

He took a break for some needed coffee, then let Sassy and Dakota out into the corral for some exercise. He wasn't sure about the fencing in the pasture, so that would have to wait until he checked it out. He cleaned out the stalls, put in new straw and made a note to pick up a few bales at the feed store in town until he could start having some delivered.

He paused, realizing he liked the physical labor, and having the horses on the ranch. Would Shelby and Ryan like that idea? He remembered how excited the boy had been to see them. Maybe he could teach the boy to ride. Whoa. Shelby should do the job.

He thought back to last night and realized he'd overreacted about the gossip. He'd heard about Bess and her eagerness to share information around town. What would Shelby do if she knew about his past? He hated how his life had changed, and even though he'd been exonerated of all charges, some people in Denver still didn't believe his innocence.

Cullen walked out of the barn as he checked his phone. There hadn't been any messages or missed calls. Okay, so everything must be fine at the office. He'd left Brad in charge, and Connie would call if there was something the lieutenant couldn't handle.

So stop worrying. That wasn't so easy for him.

He heard a vehicle and looked toward the road to see Trent's truck coming up the drive, pulling the familiar trailer. He parked next to the barn. His brother got out, and he went to the backseat and lifted his son, Chris, out of the safety seat. Cullen grinned at the chubby toddler.

"Hey, what are you doing here? Seeing if I remember how to care for animals?" He reached out and tickled his nephew. "Hi, Chris."

The boy gurgled at him and grinned, showing off two

front teeth. Then he hugged his daddy's neck, and envy sliced through Cullen.

Trent spoke, "Just thought I'd bring over a few bales of straw. Wasn't sure what was here."

"Not much," Cullen offered.

"Also I brought a saddle horse for you to ride. Danny Boy."

"What? Another horse?"

"You can't ride these older horses, not for any distance."

Cullen shook his head. What was Trent up to?

He pulled a piece of paper out of his pocket. "I've made a list of what we need for these two. I guess I should add more since you brought a third horse."

Trent reached for it, and Cullen pulled it back. "Just hold on."

"I told you I'd pay for the upkeep of the animals," Trent said.

"Don't see why we can't share." He had money from a year's back pay and the sale of his town house. "After all I'm living here for free."

Trent's eyes narrowed. "This ranch is partly yours. I have enough to do at my place, but I want to keep the Circle R in the family."

"Horsey," Chris announced.

"Yes, horsey," Cullen mimicked. "I guess we need to go see what you brought me."

The three of them headed to the trailer. Cullen released the gate, and started up the ramp. He ran a soothing hand over the horse's rump, unfastened the lead rope, then backed him out. Once on the ground, he looked over the big chestnut gelding.

He rubbed the horse's muzzle, and in return he got a friendly nudge. "Hey, big guy. You want to hang out here with me for a while?" The animal whinnied and bobbed his head.

"You'll be doing me a favor, Cullen. I can't give this guy enough attention right now."

Cullen whistled and the two other equines came immediately. The toddler didn't hesitate putting his hands on the horses as they arrived at the fence.

"How did these two do last night?" Trent asked.

Cullen shrugged. "I checked on them about ten last night, and they seemed fine."

Trent nodded toward the two rescues. "Danny can go in with them. I had them in the same corral at my place. They got along fine."

Cullen unlatched the gate, then released the lead rope for the chestnut to join the others. The animal ran off, and Cullen went to stand beside Trent at the railing. He reached out and rubbed the mare's head, then he gave Dakota a turn and his gelding blew out a long breath.

Chris laughed. "Nose."

"Yes, that's his big nose," his daddy said.

Trent looked at Cullen. "It's a shame these beauties were just discarded."

"I know. I was going to put a saddle on one to see how they do. I thought I'd wait for Shelby to get home. She was raised on a farm and used to ride."

"So how was dinner last night?"

Here it comes. "Good. Shelby's a great cook."

"I wasn't talking about the meal, I was talking about the woman."

"And her child. Remember there's a little boy around."

Trent grinned as he motioned to his son. "Yes, I know, but Brooke and I have become experts on how to get time together with a child in the house."

"Okay, I'll admit Shelby Townsend is attractive, but

she's our tenant. And she has a child to raise. Besides, my job here is temporary. So why would I act on an attraction?"

Trent grinned. "So you admit you like her?"

"I'm not blind, or immune to her beauty. I'm just not in a position to start up anything right now." He remembered too well how his last relationship went south fast during his legal troubles.

"You're going back to Denver? And your old job?"

"I didn't say that, but it's hard to give up a ten-year career."

"You don't have to tell me. Try leaving the army."

Cullen nodded. "I don't know what I'm going to do, except drive to work tomorrow and do my job."

AT FOUR O'CLOCK, Shelby pulled into the driveway. Although tired after her long day, she smiled on seeing the horses in the corral. Okay, she was excited about the possibility of going for a ride. And maybe she could introduce Ryan to that same love of horses. By the way he acted yesterday he seemed to have no fear. She was happy he wanted to try something new.

"I want to see the horses," Ryan said from the backseat.

"Honey, they aren't our horses. They belong to the sheriff."

"Can I pet them?"

She turned off the engine and looked at the horses longingly. They brought back good memories from her childhood. The carefree days of her and Georgia living on a Kentucky farm with animals to care for. It seemed like a lifetime ago.

"We'll see." She knew she needed to let the child run around. He'd been confined all morning.

Bess was right. She needed to put him in some sort of preschool. He'd only turned five just last month. He hadn't gone to kindergarten yet, and next fall would be soon enough. Yet, she wasn't sure if the child could adjust to a traditional school. Georgia had handled all his special needs. She needed to call Saint Theresa's and see if its day care program would take Ryan. She hated to leave him, but what choice did she have? Could Ryan handle the separation?

She got out of the car as Cullen came out of the cottage. "Sheriff!" Ryan called.

Cullen smiled and waved. Before Shelby could exit the car, he had the back door open and was removing Ryan from his safety seat.

"Someone else moved in to the barn today."

"A horse," Ryan said.

"Yep, and another horse."

He set the boy down on the ground. "Hi, Shelby," he said, then turned back to Ryan. "This one I can ride."

Ryan looked at her, his eyes wide with excitement. "Can I see it?"

She looked at her handsome landlord, feeling her own excitement growing. "Only if I get to come along."

"Sure." He held out a hand and Ryan took it. She was surprised how trusting her nephew had become with Cullen.

"Let's go," he said. "His name is Danny and he's playing with Dakota and Sassy in the corral." He looked over his shoulder at her and winked. "Come on, Aunt Shellie."

She suddenly realized how quickly this man was becoming a part of their lives. She followed, knowing she couldn't disappoint the child, but praying she wasn't making a mistake.

At the corral fence, Cullen lifted the boy to the railing. He was a slight child and small for his age. He got tickled, and his eyes widened when he saw the horses.

"Watch this." Cullen put his fingers in his mouth and let go with a sharp whistle.

Suddenly Ryan covered his ears and let go with a cry, then the boy buried his head in Cullen's shoulder. "Oh, Ryan, I'm sorry. I didn't mean to scare you." He rubbed his back as his aunt came up to them.

"Ryan, are you okay?"

The boy lifted his head and nodded. She looked at Cullen. "It's a sensory issue. Loud sounds are even louder for him."

"Hey, buddy, I won't do it again. I promise."

Ryan smiled. "Okay." He turned to the three horses as they came to the fence to see him.

"See this one? His name is Danny Boy."

The child seemed to recover from the incident. "He's big," the boy said and pulled back.

"But he's friendly, too." Cullen pulled a carrot out of his pocket. "Here, feed him this."

Shelby stepped up to the railing. "Watch." She laid the carrot across her palm, and Danny quickly snatched it up and Ryan laughed.

"I want to do it."

Cullen reached inside his jacket and pulled out an apple. "Try this one." He held his hand flat with Shelby's help, and Dakota took it.

The boy giggled. "Tickled."

"Yeah, horses have whiskers," Cullen explained.

Ryan looked at him. "You have whiskers." He ran his tiny hands over Cullen's day-old beard.

"Ryan, don't do that."

"It's okay," Cullen said. "He just wants to feel what it feels like."

"Does this tickle?" Cullen leaned forward and rubbed his face gently against the boy's cheek.

"Tickles," Ryan confirmed as he laughed and pulled away.

Cullen paused, suddenly feeling a connection to this child. He wasn't sure if it was good or bad. Right now he was feeling pretty good.

"Hey, how would you two like to go with me to dinner? Trent raves about Joe's Barbecue Smokehouse."

He saw Shelby tense at his invitation. "Look, you've done all the cooking so far, and brought me cookies. I'd like to repay the favor. And I hate to eat alone."

Ryan tugged on Shelby's arm. "Please, Aunt Shellie, I want to go with the sheriff."

Cullen turned to her. "Yeah, please, Aunt Shellie. Come with me to dinner."

"Okay, but the food better be good. I make a pretty good bourbon sauce for my ribs."

"You can exchange recipes with Joe." He raised an eyebrow. "I'm just hungry."

"And I'm hungry, too." Ryan said.

"I guess I'm outnumbered. So let's go."

Chapter Six

An hour later, Cullen held the door open, allowing Shelby and Ryan to walk inside Joe's Barbecue Smokehouse. A spicy aroma greeted her, along with loud voices of the many patrons. Families filled large picnic-style tables and high-back booths.

Shelby was intrigued to find the large restaurant was crowded for the middle of the week. She wanted to find out if the food was really as good as Cullen had raved about. Although she was a little more nervous about meeting up with Trent and Brooke than having someone show her up with better rib sauce.

She placed her hands on Ryan's shoulders, feeling him tense. She gave him a reassuring squeeze, letting him know she was close by.

Her nephew turned to her and tugged on her sweater. "I don't like barbecue."

She bent down. "Remember, Cullen said they have other food. But maybe you should try something new."

Ryan relented, "Okay."

A young hostess appeared. "Sheriff, your party is already here. Follow me."

Cullen came up behind Shelby. "Come on, they have a table ready for us." He placed a hand against her lower back as if it were the most natural thing to do and escorted her through the rows of tables. Several patrons greeted him. He acknowledged everyone, but kept moving. It seemed the good-looking sheriff had become popular in the short few weeks he'd been in town.

They reached an opening into the tavern, where a long wooden bar was lined with patrons, watching the several televisions playing different sports games. You could also hear in the background the familiar voice of Luke Bryan singing "Country Girl."

They came to another doorway and went inside. Seated around a long table were Trent and Brooke Landry and their son, Christopher. But there were more people, too.

Trent stood with a bright smile. "Good, you made it." He came over to them. "Nice to see you, Shelby and Ryan. You're in for a treat tonight."

"So I heard," she said, then looked at Cullen. "You didn't tell me we'd be crashing a party."

An innocent smile appeared on his face. "It isn't a party, Shelby. Just some family and a couple of friends."

A cute little girl with curly blond hair walked up to them dressed in a white T-shirt with sparkles that said I'm a Cowgirl and a pair of jeans tucked into red boots. "Hi, I'm Addy and I'm six years old. My mommy is married to my daddy." She pointed to the table. "That's them over there. Mommy is going to have two babies. They're in her tummy right now, but in three more weeks they're coming out. I get to help name them, too."

Another handsome man with dark hair came over. "Addy, I think that's enough information."

The little girl looked up at her dad. "I just want to be Ryan's friend."

Shelby kept a secure arm on Ryan as he turned his body toward her. Meeting strangers had always been difficult for him. "And I'm sure he would like that, too."

The man looked at Cullen. "Sheriff, good to see you."

"Hi, Kase. Kase Rawlins, I'd like you to meet Shelby Townsend and her nephew, Ryan."

The man turned to Shelby. "We send our daughter on ahead as the icebreaker. It's nice to meet you, Shelby. Hi, Ryan. I'm Kase, and Addy has been waiting to meet you."

"Hi, Addy," Ryan managed to say.

Kase motioned to the other blonde at the table. "Come on over and meet my wife," he said.

They approached the table and Brooke spoke, "Shelby, I hope you don't mind that we horned in on your dinner, but we all want to welcome you and get to know you better."

"It was kind of you to invite us," Shelby said.

Cullen pulled out chairs for her and Ryan. "Don't look so worried, they're harmless. Well, most of the time." He winked at her.

"It was our idea," the very pregnant woman added. "Brooke and I decided it would be nice to go out." She rubbed her expanded belly. "I'm going on house arrest next week, and I've been craving Joe's barbecue ribs. Hi, I'm Laurel. I'm married to Kase, and I'm Addy's mother and very soon adding two more to the mix."

Shelby began to relax. "I'm Shelby and this is Ryan. We're a little overwhelmed to see y'all here."

Brooke waved. "You'll get used to us, Shelby. We're pretty harmless. This is our son, Chris." She motioned to the blond-haired toddler in a high chair, grinning and drooling.

Cullen placed his arm across the back of Shelby's chair and leaned closer to her. "They're just family," he said. She inhaled his familiar scent and felt reassured just by his presence. "As you can probably tell, Brooke and Laurel are twins."

Shelby nodded. "Yes." She'd heard their story. How the two sisters found out about each other only a few years ago when their biological mother confessed about her twin's existence to Brooke.

The sisters exchanged a glance, and Brooke said, "If you work for Bess, I'm sure she's filled you in on our story. Welcome to small-town living."

Shelby blushed. "Only that you two just recently met each other."

Brooke shook her head. "It's fine. Pretty much everyone knows about us." She glanced down at her niece beside her, then to her son. "We only worry about anything said that would hurt the little ones. Believe me, there's been a lot of turmoil in this family. Somehow we've managed to survive it all, find the love of two good men and build a life here."

Shelby wasn't sure if she could find all that. But at the very least, she hoped to make a life for her and Ryan. She put on a smile. "I think it's wonderful that you two found each other." She thought about Georgia, and how many years they'd been apart, and when they finally found each other only to have her die. She touched Ryan's back. "Sometimes it's nice to go to a place where no one knows you."

Addy spoke up. "I didn't know Papa Gus until we moved to his ranch and Daddy found my new mommy."

Kase pulled Laurel closer. "Yeah, Laurel gave me a second chance and took on a ready-made family, and now we're adding to that."

"Yeah, two more at a time," his wife said.

Laughter rang out, and Shelby liked that she and Ryan were being included in this group.

The owner, Joe, appeared at the table. "I hear we have someone famous here tonight. Sous-chef Shelby

Townsend." He looked at her, and she couldn't help but blush. "Word around town is you've been cooking up a storm over at B&B Café."

The man was good-looking, especially with the mischievous look in his dark eyes. This small town seemed to be filled with an array of handsome men.

"Guilty." She wasn't shy about her cooking skills. "And I've heard your ribs are pretty good, too."

That caused a rumble around the table. "Sounds like a challenge, Joe," Trent said.

Joe grinned. "I think I'm up for it."

Shelby smiled sweetly. "Good, because Ryan and I brought our appetites."

Ryan remained silent as his legs were swinging back and forth under his chair.

"Do you like ribs, Ryan?" Joe asked.

The boy shrugged. "I like chicken."

Trent jumped in and said, "Let's stop fooling around and get to eatin'." The group placed their orders. Shelby relied on Cullen's suggestions about getting a sampler platter. And the kid's menu had several choices for the picky eaters like Ryan.

After the drinks were delivered the conversation began with questions to her. "Shelby, since you have a job at the café, will you be staying?" Laurel asked.

Cullen felt her tense, and he couldn't help but wonder why.

"I'm still trying to figure that out. Coming to Hidden Springs was only supposed to be temporary. So we'll see how it goes."

"That's kind of Cullen's attitude," Trent said. "He never stops reminding me that he's the interim sheriff."

"That's because I am," Cullen said. "Ted is coming back to work."

Trent frowned. "That's to be seen," he said in a low voice. "The man should retire."

Cullen didn't want to talk about his job situation. Not tonight. He wanted some downtime and to enjoy the company.

Laurel quickly changed the subject. "I hear you picked up some four-legged boarders at the Circle R," she said.

"Yeah, Trent didn't think I had enough to do, so he sent over a few horses."

"You had an empty barn," his stepbrother said. "All you need to do is feed them in the morning and at night and give them a little love in between." Laughter rang out. "Even a hard-nosed cop can handle that."

Cullen tensed. He knew Trent was teasing him, but he didn't want to be reminded of his past career. "Just so long as you come by and muck out the stalls."

Another round of laughter, then Laurel said, "How many empty stalls do you have?"

"Should I be afraid to answer this?" Cullen frowned, then admitted, "Four that are in decent shape."

Laurel smiled sweetly. "In my condition, I haven't been able to do much riding lately." She rubbed a hand over her expanded belly. "I'm worried about some of my horses getting enough exercise. I have this gray gelding named Cloud. In his day, he used to compete in reining shows. He's well trained and such a sweetheart." The pretty blonde gave him a pleading look. "He'd be the perfect horse for Ryan."

That got both Shelby's and the boy's attention. "Ryan's never ridden before," Shelby said.

"Do you have anything against him learning?" Laurel asked.

Shelby shook her head. "No, but he's never been around horses."

"I wish I could help," Laurel said. "But I'm going to be out of commission for a while."

"At least two months," Kase said and leaned over and kissed his wife. "Your right-hand man, Chet, will just have to take over everything." He looked at Shelby. "As if two babies and a six-year-old aren't enough to handle. Plus her horse training business."

"I'm going to help Mommy, too," Addy said.

Everyone chuckled. "Of course you are, sweetie." Laurel hugged her stepdaughter.

Cullen knew that Laurel loved Addy as much as if she'd given birth to her. The woman stepped in after Kase's estranged wife died. She helped him fight for custody of Addy from her maternal grandparents.

The conversation stopped as a parade of waitresses carried in the platters of beef and pork ribs. Soon everyone concentrated on eating.

Cullen watched as Shelby got Ryan's food arranged for him. The boy was eating French fries and chicken strips. At least there was Joe's barbecue sauce for dipping.

She turned to Cullen and brushed her hair back behind her ear, giving him a view of her pretty face. "Sorry, he has trouble trying new things."

"Don't apologize." Cullen smiled as he inhaled the soft scent of her perfume. Damn. If he wasn't careful, he could really like this woman. Whom was he kidding? He already liked her. "He'll come around."

He turned to his food and began to eat. The ribs were mouthwatering, but he found the company was even better. He glanced around the table at his brother and his family. Little Christopher was gnawing on a rib bone while Addy ate her food. Their parents were enjoying a closeness that he envied. For the first time in a long time, he wondered what it would be like to have the same thing. Could he really make a place here in this town?

Suddenly little Addy climbed up on her knees, picked up one of her ribs and reached across the table. "Here, Ryan, try this. Don't you know all cowboys and cowgirls eat ribs?"

The adults froze, then watched as the boy took the offered rib and took a small bite. He continued to eat all the meat off the bone.

"See, I knew you'd like it," the little girl said, and everyone laughed. "Don't you, Ryan?"

With barbecue sauce smeared across his mouth, the boy grinned at everyone. Another milestone.

AT DAYBREAK THE next morning, Cullen was out feeding the horses. He put Dakota and Sassy out in the corral, then headed back to the house to shower for work when his cell phone rang.

He looked at the caller ID and hesitated, seeing his father's name. He'd been ignoring Neal Brannigan's calls for the past two weeks.

"Might as well get it over with," he grumbled as he punched the answer button. "Hello, Dad."

"Well, it's about damn time you took my call."

Cullen wasn't going to let the man bait him into an argument. He walked in the back door to the house. "I've been busy, trying to get situated in my new job."

"Hell, that isn't a job. You're just babysitting those deputies until the real sheriff returns."

"If you say so."

"Of course I say so. Cullen, you need to stop messing around and come back to Denver. Your career depends on it."

"Career? What career, Dad?"

Cullen went to the coffeemaker, grabbed a mug and poured some fresh brew.

"You've got to forget about the past and start over. Maybe go to work in a new department."

For the past five years, Cullen had worked in the white-collar crimes unit. A year ago, his cover and credibility had been blown when incriminating evidence showed up against him. "What should I do, go out and work patrol again? I'm not going to do that."

"Look, son, you've been cleared and reinstated. You could go into any department."

"Yeah, like anyone would trust me, and that includes you."

He heard his father sigh. "I've already apologized for that. Besides, even you have to admit the evidence was pretty damning."

Cullen felt a familiar ache in his chest. Nothing he'd done was good enough. "What about your own son, Dad? You couldn't take his word?"

He had idolized this tough father and cop, even followed a career into law enforcement. He only wanted to make Neal Brannigan proud. "It hadn't mattered about anyone else. I only needed you to believe me."

"I had to stay neutral, Cullen. My reputation was at stake."

He couldn't deal with this right now. "Yeah, heaven forbid that you lose anything, but it would be okay if your son went to prison for crimes he didn't commit."

There was only silence on the line.

"Look, I gotta go." Cullen hung up and cursed for letting his father get to him. He should be used to Neal Brannigan's tougher-than-nails attitude. The man raised his boys that way. No matter how hard he and Austin worked and accomplished things growing up, the man wanted even more from them. Austin had the right idea. He didn't worry about his father's opinion. He didn't stay in one spot long enough to be bothered by their father. He traveled the country on the rodeo circuit.

"I'm done with you, too, old man."

"Excuse me."

Hearing the feminine voice, Cullen swung around to find Shelby standing in the doorway. She looked fresh and pretty dressed in her jeans and blouse. Her rich brown hair was pulled back into a ponytail. She was ready for work at the café.

"Sorry, I knocked, and I heard you…" She paused. "I just wanted to tell you that…never mind." She frowned. "I can see that this isn't a good time. I'll come back later."

When she started to leave, he hurried after her. "Wait." He caught her hand. "Don't go, Shelby. It's not you. In fact you're just what I need right now." When he tugged on her hand, it caused her to stumble right into his arms. He caught her surprise, her rapid breathing, but more than that, those blue depths held passion. And he wanted her.

"Cullen?"

Her saying his name broke the last of his resistance. He lowered his head and bushed his lips across hers. He was quickly becoming lost. His mouth moved over hers gently, and when she didn't show any resistance, he wrapped his arms around her back and held her close.

Oh, God. She felt wonderful. Her taste, her softness and that sexy body… He tilted her head, getting a better angle to deepen the kiss. She moaned and her hands moved to his chest, and he burned. He wanted more. He cupped her face and drank from her, his tongue moving against hers, tasting her sweetness, mixed with the mint flavor of her toothpaste.

Reluctantly he ended the kiss and released her. He

watched her blink those startling-blue eyes, and he almost went back for more. Instead, he slipped his hands into his pockets and said, "Wow! I didn't mean to do that... Did you want to ask me something?"

She opened her mouth and paused as if to clear her head. "Uh, I just was going to offer to help you with the horses." She couldn't look him in the eyes. "Look, I should go. Ryan's in the car."

He started to argue. "Okay."

She nodded. "I'll see you later." She turned and walked out the back door. He watched her until she got into her car and drove off.

"Well, that was just great, Brannigan. Talk about over-stepping your boundaries."

How was he going to fix this?

AFTER SHELBY RELUCTANTLY left Ryan at Saint Theresa's preschool, along with several phone numbers for them to call if he needed her, she arrived at the café.

In the kitchen, she tied on her apron and began her morning prep. She liked this time getting everything ready for the day. She put together the ingredients for her hollandaise sauce, along with adding sausage to the white gravy, for one of the customers' favorites, her biscuits and gravy.

As busy as she was, she was still able to relive Cullen's kiss over and over. Whatever she thought it would be like with the man, it had been a hundred times better. She swore she could still taste him on her lips, that incredible mixture of coffee and the man. Wow. Wicked combination.

Okay, just calm down.

If Shelby knew anything, it was that she couldn't get involved with Cullen. She had trouble trusting anyone in law enforcement. She couldn't take the chance. Gil had killed her sister, but there was no way to prove it.

The last thing she needed right now was for that crazed cop to show up on her doorstep. After all, Gil had accused her of having something that Georgia took from him. That was why Shelby had to sneak out of town in the middle of the night. If Cullen had done a background check on her, it might send out a red flag, alerting Gil where she'd gone. Yes, she needed to make some money in case she had to take off again.

And a new rule. No more kissing Cullen Brannigan.

Bess walked into the kitchen and smiled. "Need any help?"

"Sure." She gave the owner a task, and Bess began to put a tray of biscuits into the industrial-size oven. "Did Ryan get settled in to school okay?"

"He seems to be doing better with the separation than I am. Of course, he already knows Addy Rawlins. She's in kindergarten, but promised to help take care of him."

They both laughed. "That child is something else."

"All I know is Ryan likes her and listens to her. Last night at Joe's, he wasn't going to try a rib, but Addy got him to."

Bess folded her arms and looked at her. "You saw the Rawlinses last night?"

Uh-oh. "Yes, I did. Trent and Cullen invited us to go. It seems that Laurel has been craving ribs."

"So you went with the entire family?"

Before Shelby could answer, the double doors opened and Bill shouted back, "Incoming customers."

"Well, we better get to work," Shelby said and turned away from any more questions.

Chapter Seven

Around four o'clock, Shelby drove back to the ranch while Ryan told her all about his first day at school. It was Addy this and Addy that. He had played with the little girl at recess and ate with her at lunch. According to his teacher, the child had taken it upon herself to be Ryan's guardian.

"You know, Ryan, Addy is in kindergarten and you won't be in that grade until next year. So you need to make some friends in your class." That had never been easy for her nephew. She prayed that he hadn't been bullied, or made fun of.

"Sister Helen took me to a boy named Noah."

Shelby glanced in the rearview mirror. "Noah?"

Ryan nodded. "He's in my class. He plays video games like me."

"That's great." She felt a sense of relief as she turned the car onto the ranch road and made her way up the driveway. She passed the main house, toward the gray-and-white cottage, and parked the car.

She smiled. This was their home…for now.

"Aunt Shellie, can we go see the new horse?"

She looked toward the corral to discover the gray horse Laurel had talked about last night had been added to the herd.

"I don't know, Ryan, maybe we shouldn't bother them right now." She also wasn't sure she needed to run into Cullen at this moment. Just the thought of the lawman's kiss sent her into a turmoil of emotions. She didn't need this complication.

Speaking of the man. She saw Cullen coming out of the barn. She couldn't help but watch his long, easy gait as he made his way across the compound toward them. His faded jeans hugged his narrow hips, and his black henley shirt seemed to embrace all those muscles along his arms and chest.

She blew out a breath to calm her racing heart and got out of the car. By the time she opened the back door, Ryan was already out of his safety seat.

"Cullen will take me to see the horses." He jumped down and took off toward the man. When Ryan reached him, Cullen lifted him up in the air. Her nephew giggled as he was swung around. She hadn't heard that wonderful sound in a very long time.

Cullen boosted Ryan up in his arms. "You have a good day at school, sport?"

The boy nodded and gave him a big grin. "I got a new friend, Noah. He's five, too."

"Hey, great." He tickled his stomach. "Noah is also pretty lucky to have you as a friend, too."

"Can I see the horses?"

Cullen enjoyed the boy's excitement. He just hoped his aunt felt the same way. After this morning, he wasn't sure she even wanted to speak to him. "Let's see what your aunt says."

He set Ryan down, then watched as the pretty brunette walked toward them. Her long slender legs, encased in jeans, had him thinking about things that had no business being on his mind right now. Like that kiss this morning. Not that he regretted it, but not the wisest move on his part. He had no business giving in to temptation. He needed to set the record straight that it wouldn't happen again.

She finally made her way to him. "Hi," she greeted him in that soft husky voice that sent a warm shiver down his spine.

"Hi."

She nodded to the corral. "I see Laurel talked you into the horse."

"Yeah, I think I need a new sign out front, Brannigan Animal Rescue." How could she look so appealing after working since dawn? "Would it be okay if I show Ryan the new boarder?"

Those sparkling blue eyes met his. "Sure."

"Yeah!" An excited Ryan ran ahead to the corral fence, leaving them alone.

"Seems you're getting a new addition daily," Shelby said.

He kept his eyes on the boy. "I think I've been had. My free house isn't so free, since I'll be feeding stock for a while."

She smiled, and his heartbeat shot off. Damn, he needed to stop reacting to her every time she smiled.

He touched her arm, to stop her. "Shelby, about this morning. I need to apologize to you. I had no business kissing you."

She folded her arms across her chest. "I just thought you kissed all random women who come to your door."

He shook his head, then caught her mouth twitch. "Not random women. Only beautiful women with big blue eyes who appear at my back door at five in the morning."

She cocked her head, and desire shot through him

again. "Cullen, I can't have a relationship right now." She glanced away. "My life has to be focused on Ryan."

He held up a hand. "I feel the same way. I'm only here for a few months. My job isn't even permanent."

She laughed. "Well, with all those complications, I'd say we don't have to worry."

He nodded, just as Ryan called to both of them.

"You want to meet the new guy?" Cullen asked.

"Sure."

They made their way to the corral fence, and he lifted the boy on the high rung of the railing so he could see. "Put your fingers in your ears, kid, so I can whistle for them."

Ryan did as he was told. Cullen turned away and let go with a sharp whistle. Soon all four horses trotted over to the railing. "They're a friendly bunch, but they won't hurt you, son." He put his hand out to slow down their eagerness.

Shelby stepped on the bottom rung, and the gray quarter horse went to her, seeking attention. "He's beautiful."

"Cloud had been a show horse. A lot of times when horses can't compete any longer, the owners don't have time to spend with them. I'm not sure how Laurel got ownership of him. He's not that old, either."

"He's gentle, too."

She asked, "Wouldn't someone want him as a saddle horse?"

"Well, for now, he has a home here. Should I get Cloud and Sassy saddled and we go for a ride?"

Twenty minutes later, with the other horses in their stalls, Cullen had saddled Cloud and Sassy and he led them out into the corral.

He smiled seeing little Ryan waiting patiently with

his aunt standing beside him. Cullen walked ahead of the mounts.

"I want you to know these two are well trained, by both voice and touch commands." He handed Sassy's reins to Shelby. "You want to try her out?"

He could see the apprehension. "You trust me with her?" she asked.

"You said you rode as a kid, so I figure you didn't forget how. Besides, I doubt this mature lady will buck you off."

She smiled. "We'll see." With reins in hand, she went to Sassy, grabbed the pommel and stuck her sneaker-covered foot into the stirrup, then climbed into the saddle. The horse shifted a little, but Cullen could see her reactions were easy and relaxed.

"Walk her around the corral," he suggested. "Come on, Ryan. It's your turn." He picked up the smiling boy and set him down in Cloud's saddle, then he quickly mounted behind him. After situating the child onto his lap, he swept the reins across the horse's neck and they turned around. "Want to go for a ride?"

"Yes. Go fast," Ryan said.

Cullen smiled, feeling the boy's slight weight against him, bringing out his protective instincts. "How about we walk first? I need to see how well Cloud likes us on his back."

"Okay." The boy waved at his aunt. "Aunt Shellie, look! I'm riding with Sheriff Cullen."

"I can see that."

Cullen watched the woman atop Sassy. She stopped and pulled out her phone. "Smile," she called out.

Cullen found he wouldn't mind smiling all day at this woman. That was good and bad. He still didn't know much about her and Ryan's situation. Only that she loved her nephew, and she could cook up a storm. All he'd heard around town were raves about her food. Maybe Shelby would stay here permanently.

The easy movement of the horse was relaxing. "How are you doing, sport?"

"Good."

He held out the reins to the boy. "You hold them. If you want to turn, move them this way, and if you want to go the other side, move this way." Cullen let go. "Now you do it."

Ryan took charge and moved the reins, and Cloud turned. Cullen couldn't help but smile as he rested his hands on his legs, ready to take control back if needed. "Good job."

Shelby rode over to them. "Well, look at you two. Ryan, you're handling Cloud all by yourself."

"Take my picture, Aunt Shellie."

Shelby bit down on her lower lip, fighting a smile. She snapped another picture. "You two look good."

She brought Sassy up beside them as they continued the slow, easy journey around the large corral. Cullen enjoyed sharing this time with aunt and nephew. After about thirty minutes, they returned to the barn.

Cullen placed Ryan up on one of the storage trunks outside Cloud's stall.

"Rules of the barn, Ryan. You never go inside the stalls without an adult. Sometimes horses get spooked and they might step on you, or kick you."

"That will hurt," the boy said.

"That's right." Cullen pulled the saddle off the horse and hung it over the railing. "Another rule. We never throw anything at animals, not even if you're just teasing."

Ryan shook his head. "No. That's mean."

"You're right. And you never want to be mean to anyone, not people or animals."

"At my old school a boy was mean to me. He said I talked funny. Mom reported him, and he got in trouble."

Cullen glanced at Shelby in the next stall. She was removing Sassy's tack, but stopped and said, "Your mom did the right thing, Ryan. Bullying is against the rules."

"And it's not nice," the boy agreed. "Makes people sad."

"Hey, let's not be sad today. You got to ride a horse." Cullen walked across the straw-covered floor, opened a bin and took out a carrot. "And give him a treat."

Cloud stuck his head over the railing on hearing the special word. They all laughed and Ryan held out the carrot. As soon as the gelding ate up the food, he proceeded to drop waste from the other end.

That caused Ryan to laugh again.

"That's another rule," Cullen said. "Be careful where you step, because your aunt won't be happy if you come in the house with horse manure on your shoes."

The boy wrinkled his nose. "Okay."

Cullen carried the saddles into the tack room, and Ryan and Shelby followed with the bridles and hung them on the wall hooks. Then they helped him feed the rest of the horses. After Ryan said good-night to all the animals, they exited the barn.

"Well, that should do it until tomorrow."

Shelby looked up at him. "I can't thank you enough for today."

Ryan tugged on his arm. "Thank you, Sheriff, for letting me ride Cloud."

He crouched down to eye level with the child. "You're very welcome. These horses like to have people visit, so I hope you'll come back and see them, with me or your aunt." He stood and turned back to Shelby. "Please, don't hesitate to come out to the barn. You know your way around animals, so I know you'll be careful, especially with Ryan."

Shelby nodded. "I appreciate your offer. We might come by." She laid a protective hand on her nephew's shoulder. "Are you working tonight?"

He shook his head. "No. I went into the office today. The deputies know how to run things without me looking over their shoulders."

Shelby started to walk away, then stopped. "Would you like to come by for dinner? I brought home some leftover meat loaf."

It would be best to stay away. "Leftovers sound pretty good to me."

"Come by in about thirty minutes," she said and turned and walked off.

Cullen watched both the boy and his aunt. Everything in him shouted to stay away, but he was so drawn to her. He thought back to his last relationship in Denver. His career as a cop pretty much had killed any kind of personal life. In the past his job had taken over most of his life. It had been what he'd worked for to be able to move up the ranks in the police department.

Maybe that was why he'd always avoided any serious involvement. He thought back to the women he'd dated. From the beginning he'd warned them of his long hours and special details at moment's notice. A casual relationship was the best he could offer.

And those women never had kids…until now.

THIRTY MINUTES LATER, music blaring from the radio on the kitchen counter, Shelby was nervous as she prepared the meal. Why had she asked Cullen to dinner again? At the time, it seemed like the right thing to do since he'd taken time with Ryan. And she liked him. What was not to like? The man was sexy as all get-out. She liked him in his cowboy gear, jeans, boots and a black felt cowboy hat. And when he had Ryan sitting in front of him in the saddle and those strong arms around the child. She got a funny feeling as the memory of their kiss came to mind.

She sighed. "As you used to say, Grandma, that man sure leaves me with a hankerin'…"

She shook her head from the distracting thought. Was Cullen Brannigan too good to be true? She thought back to what she left behind in Kentucky. Her sister and grandmother were buried there, but there weren't any other ties. There were few good memories since they discovered Georgia dead, and after Gil's threats, she couldn't stay in Dawkins Meadow. No, she hoped to leave all the bad things behind and start over, for Ryan's sake.

There was a knock on the door and she jumped. She heard Ryan running from the hall. "Sheriff's here."

She tensed in anticipation, hating that she let him affect her so much. After releasing a breath, she brushed her hair back and went out to greet the man. She stopped suddenly when she saw Cullen dressed in his sheriff's uniform.

"Hi," he said.

"Are you going in to work?"

"In a few hours," he said, as his hazel eyes held hers. "One of the deputies called in sick, so I'm going to take his shift tonight."

She couldn't seem to get her heart rate under control. "Do you have time to eat?"

He grinned at her. "Sure. I showered and dressed early because I smelled like horses."

She was going to pass out if she didn't start breathing. "We can't have that."

Ryan giggled. "I took my bath, too."

Cullen ruffled the child's hair. "You smell good, too."

"Come into the kitchen. Supper's about ready."

She nodded to the sink. "Wash your hands, Ryan."

"Yes, ma'am." Cullen took charge and they both washed up while Shelby poured milk and tossed the salad.

After drying off, Cullen helped Ryan to his seat, then waited until she sat down before taking his chair across from her. She busied herself fixing Ryan a plate, but she could sense Cullen watching her.

Ryan drew her attention. "Say grace."

"You're right, it's time to say grace." Since Ryan hadn't learned the entire prayer yet, Shelby spoke the words her grandmother had taught her as a child.

"Amen," Ryan said loudly.

Shelby picked up the bowl of mashed potatoes and handed it to Cullen. He took two spoonfuls and then two slices of meat loaf. He looked at her. "Sorry, my mouth has been watering since you invited me to dinner."

"Then go ahead and eat."

She loved hearing his words of praise as she dug in to her own food. But she wasn't nearly as hungry as she thought.

"Cullen, if you tell me the schedule you keep for the horses, I could help with feeding them."

He frowned. "You don't need to do that, really."

"I know I don't, but I'd like to help out. Your family has been so generous to us. And taking on four horses is a lot of work."

"Well, since I get off duty about five o'clock, I'll handle the feeding in the morning, and in the afternoon when you get home, I'll show you how I do everything. I've been working on cleaning the tack room. Everything needs a good cleaning, and the leather needs to be conditioned."

"It's been a while, but I think I remember how. My grandmother was strict about all the equipment being kept in good condition. The barn and tack room were cleaned and well organized, too. She'd say, 'We don't want any varmints living in here.'"

Cullen smiled. "I like your Southern drawl."

"It slips out every so often." She blushed and pointed to the bowl of potatoes. "Would you like more taters?" She turned to Ryan. "How about you, sugar? Do you have a hankerin' for more taters?"

Ryan laughed, and Cullen joined in. "She must have been something, your grandmother."

"Ivy Townsend made us the best home my sister and I ever had. We didn't have a lot growing up, but living on the farm was wonderful. All the animals, and even the chores, it was good." Shelby felt the emotions tighten in her throat. She wanted to give Ryan the same kind of life. "I still miss her."

"You have part of her with you," Cullen told her. "And you have her stories to tell Ryan."

"I just wish she could have seen him…"

Ryan reached over and patted her hand. "Don't be sad, Aunt Shellie."

She put on a smile. "Okay, I won't." She loved this little boy. "Sorry. Hey, how about some ice cream for dessert?"

After they finished the meal, Shelby took Ryan to bed. Cullen checked for monsters again, then he left the room to give her time to say good-night. With the timer set on his tablet, Shelby kissed the boy, walked out and closed the door.

She came into the small living room, where Cullen was waiting for her.

"Is Ryan settled in for the night?"

"Yes, he had a pretty busy day. Thank you for the monster check."

"My pleasure. Thank you for dinner. As usual, the food was delicious."

"I'm glad you enjoyed it."

"You saw how much I ate." He studied her for a moment, then rushed on to say, "About this morning—"

"It's okay, you don't—"

"Yes, I do need to explain. I'd just gotten off the phone with my dad. He knows just what to say to get me riled up. He was badgering me about coming back to Denver and rejoining the force."

"But you have a job here," she said.

"Exactly what I told him, but he doesn't listen."

She didn't know the entire story about this man. "So you want to go back?"

"I'm not sure, but probably not. My career is pretty much over in Denver."

She wanted so badly to ask him why, but she couldn't invade his privacy. "Well, then don't let him tell you what to do. It's your decision and your life."

He smiled. "Thank you." He didn't move. "I still overstepped this morning. I don't want you to be uncomfortable around me."

"If I was, you wouldn't have been invited for dinner."

"Good." Those gorgeous eyes watched her closely. "Just so you know, I might refrain from kissing you again, but that doesn't mean that I didn't enjoy the experience. I also can't guarantee that I won't do it again."

Chapter Eight

A week later, Shelby was at the All Occasions Catering storefront located next to the café. In the past the space had served mostly as a prep station and warehouse for their reception supplies.

Shelby planned to change that look.

She'd spent the past few days sectioning off an area with white lattice panels, and adding a small round table and two chairs. A cozy spot so couples could sample foods and cakes for their weddings. In the window she added a display of flowers and the newly printed sign for All Occasions Catering.

She walked out of the kitchen in the back with a sampler plate of hors d'oeuvres: her spring rolls, baked wontons and mini crab cakes. Her heart pounded hard as she placed the food in front of the engaged couple, Nicole and Colby.

"Since you hadn't specified exactly what you want to serve at your reception," she said, "I thought I'd get a little creative."

The future groom popped a wonton into his mouth. "I want these." He turned to Nicole. "Could we also have steak?"

His bride smiled sweetly. "Honey, do you know what

it would cost to feed steak to all your friends? Dad won't allow it."

Shelby wanted to stop this argument. "I might have a compromise." She raised a hand. "One moment, please." She hurried into the back to the large kitchen. She removed two additional sampler plates from the warmer and added a little garnish. Picking up some flatware, she brought the dishes to the table.

She stood back and checked the lovely presentation of the entrées, meat and fish. The groom sliced off a piece of meat, and began to chew. It didn't take long before his eyes rounded. "Wow, this is delicious. What is it?"

Shelby couldn't help but smile. "Roasted pork sautéed with apples, along with carrots and green beans. We could switch out one of the vegetables for potatoes if you'd like something a little more substantial." She looked at Nicole. "You have the pecan-crusted salmon, with the garlic mashed potatoes."

Shelby took notes as the couple made their choices for their menu and scheduled another appointment with Colby's mother to discuss catering the rehearsal dinner, too.

Thirty minutes later, she said goodbye to the excited couple and went through the back door to the café, where she found Bess in the kitchen going over the food supplies.

"I scheduled a wedding reception for September eighth." She handed Bess the deposit check and the signed contract.

The older woman looked over the paper. "I told you that roasted pork would be their choice, along with the wontons and spring rolls." She shook her head. "I remember a time when it was chicken or steak. My word, what's this town coming to?"

Shelby laughed. "I hope this brings in more business for you."

The older woman smiled. "For all of us. You get a commission off the catering." She cocked an eyebrow. "I hope to keep you and Ryan in Hidden Springs for a long, long time."

Shelby's thoughts turned to the sheriff who she realized had become a part of her and Ryan's life. Why couldn't she dream? "I want that, too."

THAT AFTERNOON, CULLEN had come home early from work. There hadn't been anything pressing at the station, so he'd left. After changing out of his uniform, he went out to the barn. Cleaning stalls had been his haven this past week. After a year of endless wandering, he had a renewed focus...for a short time anyway.

After letting the horses out into a small pasture for some exercise, he saddled Danny Boy. He headed out along the trail and put the gelding through a brisk run. His brother was right—the large chestnut was a good saddle horse. He slowed the animal to a walk and took the route back along the road, checking for any bad sections of fence.

He also took time to enjoy the miles of green pastures and massive mountain peaks that seemed to touch the sky. He released a deep breath, and the stress of the past week eased in his chest. Being a small-town sheriff hadn't been as intense as his work in Denver.

Maybe what he thought was a bad idea to move here might not be so terrible after all. The Circle R was a pretty piece of land. It would be nice grazing for a small cattle herd, and for horses, too. Although it had been a long time since he had lived on a ranch, he'd found he enjoyed the routine with the new boarders.

He let Danny Boy take the lead as his thoughts turned to the other boarders, especially the pretty brunette with the big blue eyes. Her being here distracted him, a lot, but he also knew she wasn't the type to have a causal fling. And that was all he was interested in.

Then there was the boy. Ryan was special in many ways, and not just the obvious. In his world of pictures and videos, he managed to connect with horses. Cullen found he wanted to help the child discover more.

At the sound of an approaching car, he looked toward the gravel road and saw the familiar compact. Shelby and Ryan were home. He waved, feeling a tightening in his middle section. No use denying that the woman got to him, and he couldn't seem to keep his distance.

Shelby pulled the car to the side of the road and got out as he rode closer.

"Hi," she called.

Another zing hit him in the chest. "Hi, yourself. How have you been? I haven't seen you in a while." He wondered if she was purposely avoiding him.

She smiled. "Busy working. I booked a wedding reception."

He braced his forearm on the saddle pommel. "That's great." He leaned down lower, pushed his hat back and saw Ryan in the backseat. "Hey, kid. How was school?"

Ryan waved. "Hi, Cullen. I played with Noah at school. He wants to go riding with me. Can he?"

"Ryan." Shelby looked embarrassed. "I told you not to ask yet."

Cullen frowned. "It's okay." He loved that the boy talked to him. "Before I say yes, we should make sure it's all right with his mother."

Ryan nodded. "Can Addy come, too?"

Cullen smiled. "Maybe, but remember Addy's mom

is going to have a baby, so she might not make it, but I can ask."

"Okay."

Cullen's horse shifted. "Why don't you do some more practicing? Come and ride back to the barn with me."

"Really?" Ryan turned to his aunt. "Can I?"

Shelby hesitated and looked at Cullen. "If you're sure. I don't want to interrupt your ride."

"I've been riding for a while. I was heading back to the barn."

"Okay." She helped her nephew out of the car.

Cullen climbed off the horse, went to the fence and lifted Ryan over the whitewashed wooden railing.

He caught Shelby's concerned look, and he resisted the urge to reach out and soothe her. "Don't worry, I've been working with Danny all week. He's got a great temperament, and he's well trained."

She nodded. "I know that you'll take care of him."

No matter what she said, he could see she wasn't convinced. "If you'd like, you could come with us. You could ride Sassy. She's in the pasture, but it shouldn't be too hard to bring her in."

Her eyes lit up. "You sure?"

"I wouldn't have asked if I didn't mean it." So much for keeping his distance. "We'll meet you at the barn." He watched Shelby get back into her car, then he hoisted Ryan up into the saddle and climbed on behind him. He handed the reins to the boy. "Okay, take us back to the barn."

The child held the leather strips securely, remembering how he'd been shown. Cullen made a clicking sound, and the horse began to walk.

By the time they got back to the corral, Shelby had

retrieved the mare, had her bridled and was coming out of the barn with the saddle.

"That was fast."

Shelby swung the saddle over the horse's back. "I am when I want to do something that's fun." She tossed the stirrup across the seat and tugged on the belly clinch, making sure it was secure.

"That should do it." She looked at him. "Unless you want to test it."

He was impressed. "You seem to be doing fine. Doesn't she, Ryan?"

At the boy's nod, his aunt sent him a big smile that had more of an effect on Cullen.

She climbed onto Sassy, tugged the reins and wheeled her mount around and followed them out of the corral. Together they followed the path along the trees and stream.

Shelby rode alongside Cullen. She knew it wasn't a good idea to get too friendly, but she wanted Ryan to have this experience. Since his mother's death, he'd had some bad moments, but Cullen and going riding were the two things that he'd focused on.

"It's a lovely day," she said to break up the silence.

Cullen looked up at the cloudless sky. "Yeah, usually spring here means thunderstorms. Of course, we always need the rain."

She enjoyed the easy sway of the horse. "I remember sitting on the porch as a kid as the rain sheeted off the roof."

"I take it you liked country living," he said.

"Yes, though it was hard work. My sister and I had a lot of responsibilities at a young age." She rested her hand on the pommel as they rode along the path. "We were three women running a farm. Grandma Ivy couldn't afford to hire anyone, so we took care of two horses, Jake and Moe, and one cow, Daisy." She smiled. "We milked the cow, collected eggs from our two-dozen chickens and we raised a few pigs to sell, or slaughter." She stole a glance at him. "Those sows were too ornery. Not friendly at all."

"And I thought my brother and I had it rough taking care of horses. We lived on a small ranch outside of Denver, while my dad worked for the force. It really wasn't a working ranch. Dad leased out most of the land for grazing."

She was curious as to why he'd been estranged from his family. "Does your brother live in Denver?"

"No, Austin travels a lot on the rodeo circuit."

"Do you stay in touch?"

He shrugged. "I guess we haven't talked in a while. My job made it difficult. Usually if I call his cell phone, he gets back to me."

"What's his event?"

"Bull rider." Cullen tossed her a sexy grin. "He's crazy. Someday he's going to get badly hurt. I think he caught the rodeo bug hearing all Trent's stories about his dad, Wade Landry, and his best friend, Rory Quinn. Rory is Brooke and Laurel's dad, and both men are National Final Rodeo champions."

Shelby enjoyed listening to Cullen talk. He seemed to be the most relaxed and open while on horseback. "So Wade Landry had once been married to Leslie?" Shelby asked.

Cullen nodded. "They divorced when Trent was about fifteen. People say it was because of Trent's brother's death. Wade blamed himself for his son's death, and the family never recovered from it. After the divorce, Leslie moved to Denver, met my dad, and the rest is history."

"It's good that you are able to reunite with Trent."

"Yeah, I'm glad I have this chance to get to spend time with him and his family."

Cullen shifted in the saddle. He wasn't crazy about talking about himself. Now that Leslie was gone, there was no reason to put up a front. He and Neal Brannigan didn't get along. God help him, he'd tried over the years.

Suddenly he noticed Danny Boy's reins had gone slack. He glanced down at Ryan to discover he was sound asleep. He quickly secured his arms around the child.

"I think we lost one."

Shelby looked over, and Cullen could see the love in her eyes for this little boy. "Poor thing, he had a busy day. I hate getting him up so early, but I don't have much choice right now."

They turned the horses around to head back to the barn. "I guess living in the country has its disadvantages," Cullen said. "Doesn't he get to nap at the school?"

"Most days." She glanced again at the boy. "Sorry, he must be heavy."

"I think I can handle his sixty pounds." Cullen tightened his arms around the child, not wanting him to fall. "Why don't we schedule Ryan's friend to come out on Saturday, or Sunday. Do you have either day off?"

"Sunday. Should we invite Addy, too?"

He nodded. "I'll check with Kase. Since Laurel is on bed rest, he might not want to leave her."

They were just about to the corral, but he noticed how quiet Shelby was. "What's wrong?"

She shook her head. "I hate taking up all your time off, Cullen. You should spend it with your family."

"I've spent more time this month with Trent than I have since we were kids. Just ask him. He was in the army for about a dozen years. He decided to retire when Wade died and left him the Lucky Bar L."

"That's quite a career change."

"Yeah. There were a lot of ghosts to exorcise when he returned home. I think Brooke coming into his life helped him a lot."

"Some memories are hard to deal with," she said, looking preoccupied with her own thoughts. He wondered again what secrets she was hiding. He hoped that one day she'd trust him enough to tell him.

"And sometimes we never get over them." Her voice grew soft. "I worry about Ryan. He's been occupied with school, but it's only been a little over a month since he lost his mother."

"You're doing a wonderful job with him."

"Thank you. I pray every day that I'm doing what's best for him."

When they reached the corral, Shelby dismounted and came over to take Ryan. Once the boy was secure in her arms, Cullen climbed off Danny. He turned back to Shelby and reached for the boy, but she resisted. "No, I'll take him."

"I can carry him to the cottage."

Shelby gave in and let Cullen take the boy from her. In the transfer, they got close, very close. The memory of how she felt being in the man's arms, her body pressed against him, caused her to shiver with awareness.

Cullen stepped back with Ryan. "If you'll tie the horses to the railing, I'll take care of them later. Then you can drive your car to the cottage."

She did as he asked. She went to her compact, drove it across the compound and parked it in her spot in the driveway. She had just unlocked the front door when Cullen followed her inside.

Silently he carried the child down the hall to the bedroom. He laid him down on the bed, then turned and left the room.

Shelby covered Ryan with a blanket and walked out. She would give him an hour to nap, not wanting him to be up late tonight.

She went out into the main room and found it empty. Feeling a little relieved, but also disappointed to find that Cullen had gone, she locked the front door out of habit and walked back to her bedroom as she began to strip off her chef smock.

She had time to take a well-deserved soak in the tub. In the closet she reached for her robe on the hook, but found it on the floor. She retrieved it, then went to the dresser for some clean underwear. She opened the drawer and found her things moved around. She froze, feeling the hair on the back of her neck tingle. Had someone been in here?

She began to look for any other signs. Her heart raced as she checked the other dresser drawers, but found nothing out of place. Back in the closet, besides the robe, everything else seemed the same. Other than her robe and the one drawer, everything looked fine. Okay, she was an organizational nut. She always had been.

In the living room, she looked around to see if anything seemed different. She saw Ryan's favorite picture book on the coffee table and smiled. She loved that he'd left the album home today.

She sat down on the sofa and opened the book. The first picture was of Ryan as a baby, and next was him with his mother. Georgia had just given birth. Shelby wished she'd been there to witness her nephew's birth, but they hadn't found each other yet.

There was one of Ryan's father in his army uniform. Lieutenant Joshua Hughes was a handsome man. Now both Ryan's parents were gone. She brushed a tear off her cheek. She missed her sister. With barely a year since they found each other, there hadn't been enough time. As bad as Georgia's death had been on her, how did a five-year-old deal with a life without his parents?

It was her job now to give him love and security. But how did she know if she was doing it right? Whom did she ask for advice? Loving the boy was easy. The other areas of raising a boy she wasn't sure about. She thought about Cullen. Ryan was getting attached to him. What if he broke the child's heart…? Or hers?

Chapter Nine

Sunday arrived and Shelby was as excited as Ryan, just not for the same reasons. She hadn't seen Cullen in the past three days, not even to exchange a casual wave. The only contact had been a message he'd left on her phone that told her to invite Noah today for one o'clock.

As she and Ryan made their way out to the barn, Kase's truck pulled up to the corral. He climbed out and helped Addy out of the backseat. Ryan took off running toward the girl, calling her name.

Shelby laughed as the two kids met. Addy immediately took Ryan's hand. "Looks like they're friends," Kase said, then he turned to her. "Hi, Shelby."

"Hi, Kase. Thank you for bringing Addy by today. I know Laurel is getting close to her due date."

The handsome man's eyebrows drew together in worry. "Yeah, she forced me to come today, said I was annoying her. I'm not allowed back for two hours, or unless she calls. Her mother is with her, so I'm not worried...much."

Shelby laughed. "Sorry, I got the picture in my head of a very pregnant Laurel pushing you out of the house."

"Hey, she bosses around two-thousand-pound stallions. You don't want to mess with her."

Cullen walked out of the barn, and the two youngsters

ran to him. The sheriff accepted their hugs, then waved to Kase and Shelby.

"It's good to see that guy happy again." Kase waved at the group. "He's had a pretty rough year."

Shelby wasn't going to ask, but she already knew it had something to do with his job in Denver. She quickly was distracted when Trent's truck pulled in. "Looks like we have more kids coming today."

The two children waved but were busy looking at the horses.

Trent walked over. "Hi, Shelby, Kase. I thought I might stop by to help you out. Brooke and Chris are on their way to your house to hang out with Laurel."

Shelby found she was a little jealous of the sisters' time together. "That's good for her to have Brooke there."

Kase jumped in, "Laurel told me to tell you she wants you, Ryan and Cullen to come by for supper tonight." He smiled. "She hopes you'll accept, because it'll be a while since the twins will be here soon."

"I'll accept, but I want to contribute something to the meal."

Kase shook his head. "No, my mother-in-law, Diane, has it all under control and Brooke's there to help, too."

"Then tell her, thank you. We'd love to come."

Trent nodded toward his brother, Cullen. "Good, because I want to see more of this guy," he said loudly.

Cullen walked over with the kids in tow. "You can come by to see me all you want, just don't bring me any more horses."

Both brothers laughed as a tan van came up the drive and parked beside the other vehicles. They all walked over to meet Noah Phelps's mother. Shelby wasn't surprised when the little boy joined Ryan and Addy, but Jeanie Phelps went inside the van and suddenly an automatic door opened, revealing another boy about ten seated in a wheelchair. Shelby was caught off guard, seeing the disabled child.

"Hi, Shelby," the older woman called as she lowered the wheelchair to the ground. "I hope you don't mind, I brought my older son, Luke, along. His father had to go out of town on business."

Shelby hoped she was able to hide her shock.

"Of course not. I just didn't know you had another child, or I would have suggested he come, too." She looked at the boy. "Hi, Luke. Glad you could come today."

Jeanie smiled. "Thank you." The mother looked at the men. "Hi, Trent. Kase, I hope Laurel is at home resting."

"She is, Jeanie. Those twins are getting more and more active. She's on bed rest."

"Good. She needs to get all the relaxation she can now." She looked at Trent. "Hi, Trent. How is that little guy of yours?"

"Growing like a weed. Jeanie, this is my brother Cullen."

Jeanie smiled. "It's nice to finally meet you, Sheriff."

"Pleasure's mine, Jeanie. I'm glad you could bring Noah by today."

"He's been so excited about his new friend."

Cullen looked at the older boy in the wheelchair. "Hi, Luke. I'm glad you could come today, too."

The boy waved his arms and made sounds, but no words.

The three other kids came running over. "Can we ride now?" Ryan asked.

"Okay," Cullen said. "I got the horses saddled, but first we need to go over some rules."

Even though Addy had ridden for the past two years, she listened intently to the instructions just as the boys did.

"Okay, let's see. Noah, you go with Trent and he'll put you on Dakota. Addy, you go with your dad and ride Sassy."

"Yeah, I love Sassy." She jumped up and down, causing her blond curls to bounce. "She's so sweet."

"And I'll take Ryan on Cloud."

Each child went with the assigned person, but this time, new helmets magically appeared with the horses. Shelby wholeheartedly approved of the added protection. Addy was already a natural on horseback, but the other two needed more instruction. Each child was on a horse, and an adult walked them around.

Shelby helped Jeanie bring her other son closer to the railing. It wasn't easy on the gravel. She felt bad that Luke couldn't also ride, but she wasn't about to say anything, knowing it probably took a special saddle to keep him upright.

She stood next to Jeanie. "I probably should have told you about my son Luke," Jeanie said. "I wasn't planning to come with him, then when John got called out of town, I didn't want to disappoint Noah."

"Of course you should have brought him."

Jeanie smiled at her. "I appreciate that. A lot of people feel awkward around a child with disabilities."

"I just think a lot of people don't know what to do, or say. Ryan has issues, too. His aren't as severe as Luke's, of course. His are social, and I'm happy that he became friends with Noah. That's a big step for him."

"Noah is a good brother to Luke, too. Sometimes he gives up so much because my attention has to be focused a lot on our other child. It's not that I have favorites, it's just the way it is when a child has special needs. This afternoon of horseback riding was to be just for Noah."

Noah waved to his brother. "Look, Luke. I'm riding a horse."

Luke raised his hand a little. Shelby smiled as she blinked back tears. Not because she was sad, but touched seeing the strong bond between the brothers.

Shelby looked at Ryan, seeing how happy he was sitting atop Cloud all by himself. He looked at her and waved, too. She pulled out her phone and began taking pictures as he walked the horse around the corral.

She focused on the handsome sheriff who turned in his badge for the day to spend time with some kids. He was one of the good guys, and she was falling for him. And there wasn't any safety net.

TWO HOURS LATER, after the rides finished, the kids helped brush and feed the horses, then the adults put them in their stalls for the night. Jeanie, Noah and Luke went home with a promise to go riding again.

At the cottage, Shelby got Ryan bathed and in a clean pair of jeans and a shirt for their trip to the Landrys' home. She hurried to get ready, too, then changed into black jeans and a royal blue sweater. After applying some makeup, she'd grabbed her purse when there was a knock on the door.

She heard the knock, then Ryan running down the hall.

Soon she heard Cullen's voice, and her stomach tightened in excitement. No denying any longer that she was glad to be spending more time with the man. In the past she'd always been able to take or leave her relationships, then walk away when it had run its course. This time was different. The handsome sheriff made it difficult to keep her distance.

She walked out to find Cullen dressed in fresh jeans and a black Western shirt. He held his cowboy hat in his hand. Her heart fluttered when he gave her an admiring look.

"Are you ready?"

Oh, boy, was she. "Just a second." She went into the kitchen and picked up the cake carrier and returned.

"I thought you weren't supposed to bring anything."

She smiled. "I made a cake for you, to thank you for today. I hope you like red velvet."

He looked surprised and maybe a little embarrassed. "I don't know if I've ever had any before. We should take it tonight."

"Yay," Ryan cheered. "It's real good."

Cullen ruffled the boy's hair. "Then we'll save you a big piece."

With Ryan taking a few of his favorite things to show Addy, they walked out the door. After transferring the booster seat from Shelby's car to Cullen's truck, they drove to the Rawlins Horse Ranch.

Shelby felt a little nervous coming here with Cullen. This was his family, and even though she knew the others, this was the second time they'd come to a social function together. Would everyone consider her and Cullen a couple?

They walked up the steps just as Kase swung open the door. "Welcome, Cullen, Shelby and Ryan. Please come in."

"Thank you." Shelby guided Ryan in first, then followed inside the large entry with the dark hardwood floors and taupe-colored walls.

"Come on, everyone is in the back of the house." Kase led them into the family room with a huge stone fireplace along with a large-screen television.

Stretched out on a camel-colored sectional sofa was

Laurel. "Good, you made it," she said. "Hello, Shelby and Ryan. Welcome to our home."

Ryan was quickly distracted by Addy. The two children took off to go play.

Laurel motioned to an older couple. "Shelby, this is my mom and dad, Diane and Rory Quinn."

Diane spoke up first. "It's so nice to finally meet you. I hear from Bess what a wonderful job you're doing at the café."

"It's nice to meet you, too, Mrs. Quinn. Bess took a chance on me. I'm glad everyone likes my cooking."

Rory leaned closer and winked. "I've sampled some of your delicious French toast."

"I'm glad you like it, Mr. Quinn."

"Darlin', you just stop with the Mister and Misses. We're just plain Rory and Diane." Rory glanced at her cake carrier. "You bring us some treats?"

"I baked a red velvet cake for Cullen, and he decided to bring it tonight." She realized what she said and felt heat rise to her cheeks. She glanced across the room at Cullen. He was talking with Kase and Trent.

Diane motioned to her. "Come, let's take the cake into the kitchen," she suggested.

They walked across the large room with more gleaming hardwood floors and into a hall. Shelby caught a glimpse of the stairs with a carved banister that led to the second floor.

"Laurel and Kase have a beautiful home."

Diane smiled. "Yes, they do. There's been a recent addition for Kase's father, Gus, and they also added a master suite after Kase and Laurel married. With the babies coming, it's good to have the added room."

"I bet you're excited about the twins, Grandma."

Diane beamed and stopped. "I'm beyond words. I

adore Chris and Addy." Her eyes got misty. "You see, Laurel isn't my biological daughter, but I love her as if she were. Then when Brooke came looking for her sister a few years ago, I wasn't exactly welcoming. But Brooke forgave me, and invited me to be Christopher's grandma."

Working for Bess, Shelby knew their touching story. "The babies are lucky, too. I know what my grandmother meant to me. I miss her."

Diane took hold of her hand. "I heard about your sister, Georgia. I'm so sorry for your loss."

"Thank you," Shelby said, her voice suddenly hoarse.

"If you or Ryan ever need anything, you have friends here."

Shelby was touched by her kindness. "Thank you."

They walked through the dining room and into a large state-of-the-art kitchen. "Wow! This is beautiful." She glanced around, from the walls of cream-colored cabinets and granite counters to the stainless steel appliances. She also caught the aroma of a spicy chili coming from the two large slow cookers.

She set the cake on the counter, and an older man came in from a pantry. "It sure is. A person has room to get around in here."

Diane did the introductions. "Gus Rawlins, this is Shelby Townsend. Shelby, this sweet man is one of the best horse trainers around."

"It's nice to meet you, Gus."

The weathered-faced man crossed the room with a slight limp. "It's nice to finally meet you, Shelby. Addy has been talking up a storm about that little guy of yours."

"Yes, they've become good friends."

Gus grinned. "I hear you're out at the Robertsons' place. Nice piece of property for horses."

She laughed. "And it seems Cullen has been collecting a few."

"I heard our new sheriff is doing double duty these days."

She nodded. "Trent and Laurel talked him into taking in a few boarders. And yes, I think Cullen enjoys having the horses around."

Diane went to the double-door refrigerator. "Would you like something to drink? There's beer, wine, soft drinks…"

"I wouldn't mind a beer."

Diane smiled. "That does sound good with chili, doesn't it?"

Laurel's mother pulled out two longneck bottles, opened them and handed her one.

"Thank you." Shelby took a drink as laughter erupted from the other room.

Diane smiled. "Come on, sounds like we're missing all the fun."

Shelby looked at Gus. "Do you want me to help with anything?"

Gus waved her off. "I know you're a pretty fancy cook and all, but my chili is legendary." He winked. "Best in the county."

Shelby smiled. "I look forward to eating some. Just holler if you need anything."

Back in the family room, everyone was gathered around Laurel. She was telling stories from her childhood.

"I used to follow after Trent whenever I could find a way," Laurel said. "I remember a time when I saw you riding with Lisa…what's her name?"

Trent groaned. "Oh, God, please save me." He gave his wife a pleading look. "I was only about fifteen."

Laurel brought the attention back to her. "Well, I caught up to them at the creek." She winked at Trent. "Let's just say I learned more about the facts of life seeing those two than I did from any of the animals on the ranch."

The room broke up into laughter, then Cullen said, "He was kind of like that when he came to Denver. I think the girl's name was Allie…" He looked at Trent, who turned to his wife.

"I swear they're making this up."

Brooke shrugged. "I guess I'm going to have to work harder at making you forget all these other women."

Trent winked at his wife and pulled her close.

Cullen watched the interaction with the families. He hadn't felt anything like this in a long time. If ever. He looked at Shelby's smiling face. Damn, she was pretty, and those big blue eyes were killing him. He was glad she was having a good time and making friends here. He couldn't deny any longer that he cared for her. That still was a problem because in about a month, he'd be out of a job. And since there weren't any law enforcement positions here, he'd have to go somewhere else for work. No good, if he wanted to start something up with the pretty chef. Hell, he was well beyond the starting point.

"Hey, Cullen," Kase called as he got up. "You want a beer?"

"Sure."

Laurel drew his attention. "I hear from Addy you had a great afternoon. Thanks for including her."

Cullen shrugged. "The kids enjoyed it."

"I hear that Jeanie Phelps brought Luke today."

He nodded. "Yeah, I only wish I could have rigged something so Luke could ride, too."

Laurel looked at him, and her pretty green eyes widened with interest. "I think I know where I can get one of those saddles. The Bradley Ranch. Joe Bradley had a stroke and lost the use of his left side, but he refused to give up riding and got a therapy saddle. I bet Alice still has it around. I'll call her in the morning."

"Whoa, slow down." Cullen raised a hand. "We can't just put a disabled child on a horse."

Laurel frowned. "Well, we can check with Jeanie and see if Luke can handle a ride. Of course you'll need a gentle horse. Sassy would work perfectly. She's the smallest we have and has the best temperament."

"We still have to be able to safely get the child on and off the horse," Cullen argued. What was he thinking? He was the sheriff, not a riding instructor.

Rory walked over and joined in. "Remember, Laurel, when you were too small to get on a horse by yourself, we built you a platform. It wouldn't be that difficult to make one again, just a little wider to handle a wheelchair."

Before Cullen knew what was happening, Trent and Rory had set up a time to bring some lumber by to help construct the ramp. "Go on without me. I'll just figure out how to protect the town in between riding lessons," Cullen said jokingly.

Trent winked at him. "Hey, you can handle it."

Cullen looked at Shelby. He wasn't sure how she felt about all this, either. It would be a commitment just to have kids over to the ranch. He was reminded of the times he'd spent at the local boys club in Denver. Working with those kids had been a special time for him, then he went undercover and he had to give it up. Seemed he'd given up a lot of his personal life for his career. And then his fellow officers turned their backs on him.

He got up, walked into the empty kitchen and took a beer out of the refrigerator. After a long pull, he leaned against the counter.

Shelby showed up in the doorway. "Is everything okay?"

He shrugged. "A few afternoons of riding seems to

have morphed into something a lot bigger. But I did hate the fact that Luke couldn't go riding today. Did you see the kid's face?"

"Yes, but he was happy for his brother. Could you even get him on a horse?"

"That's something we have to okay with Jeanie first."

Shelby crossed the room and took out a bottle of water for herself. "I feel as if Ryan and I are disturbing your sanctuary as it is. Now we've brought in more people."

"If I didn't want you there, I'd let you know."

She turned toward him. "But you never planned on renting the cottage to us."

"No, I'd probably be living in the cottage instead of the big house."

Her azure eyes rounded. "Oh, Cullen, I didn't realize. We should leave. I mean, now that I'm employed—"

"No, Shelby, you can't leave." He took hold of her hand. "I like having you there—I mean the both of you." Her hand was soft, her fingers long and slender. He didn't want to let go.

She smiled. "I like living in the country again." She looked down at their linked hands, but didn't pull away. "It's good for Ryan, too."

"Then you should stay as long as you want."

Her gaze locked on his. "I want…to stay."

Finally the sound of voices drew them apart, and Brooke and Diane came into the kitchen and began to dish out the chili. Damn, if Shelby didn't make him forget where he was.

It was nearly ten o'clock when Cullen drove Shelby and Ryan home. Home. She liked the sound of that. So much she wanted to think of the ranch as her home. She laid her head back on the seat and thought about the fun they'd had at the Rawlinses' ranch. How the family opened their home and allowed her and Ryan to share a part of their world.

"Tired?" Cullen asked.

"A little, but it was a great day, and evening." She glanced into the back at the sleeping child. "Thank you for helping make today so special for Ryan."

"Not a problem. I only saddled a few horses."

"I'm not going to argue the point, but you made three kids pretty happy."

Cullen pulled into the drive between the two houses and parked the truck. He shut off the engine, but didn't get out. "What about you? Are you happy?"

She stole a glance at him in the dark cab. "Yes. These past few weeks have been incredible. Moving here, finding a job and a school for Ryan. It's important to me that he get settled in and be comfortable here."

"I'm glad you're settling in, too." He reached for her hand to bring her across the seat.

She was settling in more than she should be, but she couldn't seem to stop herself. She wanted to stay here and build a life.

When Cullen reached for her hand and tugged to bring her across the bench seat, she didn't resist. "The one problem is, you're distracting me, Miss Shelby." She felt his breath across her check, and her heart began racing. She should push him away, but she couldn't. She wanted this too much.

Cullen's hands reached behind her neck, tipped her head back, then his mouth closed over hers. She moaned as his lips caressed hers. She wanted to savor the feeling, the taste of the man's hunger. Her arms moved around his shoulders and she shifted closer, closer to his heat, to his strength. As his mouth caressed hers, his hand went to the front of her shirt and touched her breasts through her sweater. She arched her back, pressing against his palm, and released a groan. He broke off the kiss and shifted his lips to her ear. "I can't seem to keep my hands off you, from kissing you," he whispered. "And I want to do more."

"I want that, too."

He smiled against her mouth. "And there doesn't seem to be anything we can do about it right now."

She released a breath of frustration, and he kissed the end of her nose.

"I better get you and Ryan inside."

He flipped a switch to keep the interior light off when he got out of the truck. Shelby blew out a breath and climbed out the passenger side. With Cullen carrying Ryan, they made their way up the path to the door. That was when she noticed the porch light was off, then she saw that the door was ajar.

This time her heart raced for a completely different reason. "Something's wrong," she said, thinking of the worst-case scenario. Gil Bryant.

"Did you forget to close the door?"

In the silence, he could hear her heart pounding in her chest.

"Come with me," Cullen said under his breath, and Ryan stirred in his arms. He transferred the boy to his shoulder, then grabbed for Shelby. "Let's get out of here."

Shelby followed Cullen's quick steps to the main house. On the porch, she took Ryan as Cullen pulled out his keys and unlocked the door. Inside, he didn't turn on any lights. He just went to the hall closet and took out a gun. "Don't let anyone in."

He took off, and Shelby wanted to call him back. She didn't want him hurt because of her. She held on tight to Ryan. Her nightmare had come true. Gil had found her.

Chapter Ten

Gun drawn, Cullen worked to control his breathing as he slowly pushed open the cottage door. He wasn't sure if anyone was still there, but he was going to be prepared to handle any threat to Shelby and Ryan.

Only the outside light illuminated his way through the living room. So far, nothing looked to have been disturbed. He continued his journey.

He glanced into the kitchen and saw two cupboard doors askew. Suspicious. He doubted Shelby left her kitchen any way but immaculate.

He stepped over a tiny metal car on the floor and made his way down the hall. After checking the empty bedrooms and bath, he concluded there wasn't anyone in the house. He holstered his firearm and turned on the overhead light. He tried to stay professional, but it was difficult. Just about everything from his training told him someone had been here. Since Shelby's sister's murder was unsolved, there could be someone after her, too.

He looked around, but nothing seemed to be damaged. He couldn't even call it in. There was no sign of a forced break-in, but he knew in his gut someone had been in this house. And he was going to find out who that was.

Careful not to touch anything, he left and walked back to his house. Inside, the kitchen was empty, and when he went into the dark family room, the kitchen light showed Ryan asleep on the sofa and Shelby standing by the fireplace.

He motioned her into the kitchen. She looked frightened, but he ignored it as she walked past him.

He blew out a breath. "I think it's time you tell me what the hell is going on."

She nodded as her trembling hand brushed her hair back.

"Two questions. Who's after you? Does this have anything to do with your sister's murder?"

He could see the fear in her wide eyes. "I don't have any proof, but yes, I believe it's the man who killed Georgia."

Cullen tried to remain calm, but how could he when a possible murderer was threatening her? "Who would that be?"

"Detective Gil Bryant, Dawkins Meadow Police Department."

Cullen didn't quite know what to say. He directed her to the table. "Sit down and start at the beginning."

She took a seat. "Two years ago, my sister, Georgia, began dating Gil Bryant. He was the first man she'd dated since her husband, Josh Hughes, died overseas.

"At first she liked Gil, but when she discovered he was following her everywhere, and questioning her about her friends, she broke off the relationship. But he refused to let her go. He had her watched all the time, and even became abusive."

He tensed. "Did she call the police?"

Shelby nodded. "Yeah, she did, but his fellow officers took his side. So it ended up being her word against his. Since she was afraid of losing her teaching job, she didn't press the issue." She looked at Cullen. "I wasn't there to witness any of this. At the time, I was working a few hours away in Louisville."

Shelby wiped away a tear that escaped down her cheek, unable to tell if Cullen believed her. "Georgia and I had lost track of each other for years. After Grandma died, they separated us when we got put into foster care. We'd only found each other last year. When I learned about her trouble with Gil, I tried to help her. I wanted to bring her and Ryan to Louisville, but Gil had a long reach.

"Georgia discovered that he and his cop friends had been watching the house. That was when she learned about his drug connections. She didn't want me to know too much, but from what I gathered, Gil and another police officer were taking money and it involved drugs." She shook her head. "I don't know much more. Like I said, Georgia didn't want me involved in the mess."

Cullen sat there a minute, then asked, "Did she say anything about having some incriminating evidence?"

"No. And that's what I told Gil when he asked me."

Cullen frowned. "When did you talk to him?"

"At the funeral, Gil approached me and said that Georgia had something of his and he wanted it back."

She blew out a breath. "All I knew was that Georgia wanted Ryan away from that man. She'd wanted to make a new life here in Hidden Springs. I was going with them. The plan that day was for me to pick Ryan up at school, and we had a meeting place in a strip mall. She'd leave her car there in the parking lot, and we'd make our escape in my compact. When she didn't show, I knew something was wrong. I took Ryan to the babysitter and drove by her house."

Shelby shivered, recalling the scene. With Cullen's nod, she continued on. "There were police cars everywhere. They said she'd been shot and killed due to a break-in.

Of course, Ryan and I stayed in town long enough to bury her. The funeral costs took a lot of the money that we were going to use to relocate. After the service, Gil came to me and said Georgia had something that was his, and he wanted it back. I knew I had to keep Ryan safe. Since the Donaldson cook's job was still available—" she looked Cullen in the eyes "—or I thought it was, I stuck to the plan and came here. I hoped that Gil would leave us alone."

Cullen paused, trying to piece together her story. "Did the police ever find any connection to the killer and your sister?"

She shook her head. "You can look at the police report. If you already have, maybe that alerted Gil on where to find us."

Cullen folded his arms over his chest. "I ran a check on you. I looked up the investigation on your sister, but I didn't contact Dawkins Meadow police." Why did he feel guilty then? Maybe Bryant got a hold of her sister's phone and checked the numbers.

"I guess it doesn't make any difference now." Shelby sighed. "He's found us."

"You don't know that. There's nothing in the cottage that shows evidence of a break-in."

She gave him a stern look. "I don't leave my doors open."

He knew that. Someone had been inside the house, but he wasn't going to frighten her.

She looked at Cullen. "The cottage is a mess, isn't it? Did he damage the structure?"

"There isn't any damage. Besides, I couldn't care less about the property," Cullen said and reached for her hand. "It's you and Ryan that are important."

"Thank you, but we can take care of ourselves."

She swallowed hard, unable to look him in the eyes.

She'd been on her own a long time. "If you'll give me a few hours, we can be packed and move out." God, she didn't want to leave. "I'll pay you until the end of the month."

With a curse, he stood and paced the length of the kitchen, then came back to her. "You're not going any-where, Shelby. If there is a rogue cop looking for you, you'll be safer here. So get any idea out of your head about leaving."

Shelby looked at him. She couldn't let her guard down even when he was offering to help her. It was hard for her to trust. The one person she'd loved and trusted had been taken from her. She couldn't endanger anyone else. "But he could hurt your family."

"Not if we stop him first."

"But he's a cop."

Cullen couldn't understand why she felt that made a difference. His protective instinct kicked in, and he knew he had to protect Shelby and Ryan. "That doesn't automatically make him innocent." He had his own ex-perience with a crooked partner. "In my opinion he's guilty because he put his hands on your sister. He's an abuser. That alone should make him the first suspect in her death. Did they give you any idea who they thought would come in and shoot Georgia?"

She shrugged. "They said she probably surprised a robber."

Yeah, that was a typical answer. "Who's heading the investigation?"

"I talked to a Captain Kershaw."

He was going to make a few calls himself in the morn-ing. "Look, we're all exhausted. Why don't I take Ryan upstairs to bed?"

She looked surprised. "You want us to stay here?"

He nodded. "You're not going to be left alone until I make sure it's safe. I'll check out the cottage in the daylight and install security."

He reached for her, and when she didn't resist, he drew her against him. "You and Ryan need to be here, Shelby," he whispered. "I won't let anything happen to either of you." He closed his eyes, relishing the feel of her in his arms.

Damn, if he hadn't just made a commitment.

TWO HOURS LATER, Shelby stood outside the same bedroom that Ryan had slept in that first night they arrived here. The bed was still made up. After Cullen had carried her nephew upstairs, she'd removed his shoes and jeans, then slipped him under the covers with only a few grumbles. She sat on the edge of the bed and watched Ryan's even breathing. He'd been so happy these past few weeks. Now she might have to upset that calm again.

How could she tell him that they might have to leave here and find another place to live? Even though Cullen offered them a safe haven, she was so afraid that he'd get hurt in the cross fire.

With a soft kiss on the boy's head, she left the room and walked across the hall to the other bedroom.

She knew she shouldn't have gotten so comfortable in this town. Everything was too perfect. And from past experiences, she had trouble trusting that feeling. After kicking off her shoes, she lay down on the comforter, hoping that she would be able to get a little sleep. But how could she?

The sound of the back door opening and closing alerted her someone was in the house. She went out into the hall and was relieved to see Cullen coming up the stairs.

She relaxed, but he saw her fear.

He wrapped her in his arms. "You're safe here, Shelby."

She couldn't let Cullen be responsible for them. She stepped back. It was her job. She'd promised Georgia. "Did you find anything more at the cottage?"

"No." He handed her a bag. "I gathered some clothes and things for tonight."

She smiled. "You brought his tablet?"

He nodded and Shelby fought to keep from breaking down at his thoughtfulness.

Cullen walked into her bedroom, then closed the door so they wouldn't disturb Ryan. He sat her down on the bed. "It's going to be okay, Shelby. We'll figure this out."

"Georgia thought she could handle him, and it got her killed. Both Ryan's parents are gone now. I'm all he has left. If Gil gets to me, he will be left with no one."

Cullen walked across the room. He wished he could take away her fears. "That's not going to happen. You're going to be around for a long time to raise that little boy. You're going to stay in town and build up your business." He found he didn't want her to disappear from his life, either.

She raised her head. "How can you promise that?"

Time to step up to the plate, Brannigan. "For one thing, I've had a few years' experience with scum like Bryant. Secondly, there must be something pretty important for him to come all this way. We just need to find it." He paused a moment, then asked, "Your sister didn't talk about a key or a diary with information?"

Shelby shook her head. "She never mentioned anything. I think she was trying to protect us."

Cullen knew a lot of abuse victims kept things to themselves. He was going to do his own investigation on Detective Gil Bryant first thing tomorrow. "Let's not think about this any more tonight. Try to get some sleep." He started for the door.

She stopped him. "Cullen, I hate to ask, but would you have a T-shirt?" She held up the bag. "You brought me some clothes, but nothing to sleep in."

The thought of her wearing nothing but a thin shirt caused him to swallow. "Sure."

She followed him down the hall to the master bedroom. He hadn't done anything to this room besides moving in his clothes. He turned on the overhead light, showing off the huge four-poster bed and handmade quilt pushed to the end, exposing the crumpled sheets. "Sorry, I'm not the best housekeeper."

"I could help you with that if you like."

He paused at the dresser. "You don't need to clean my house, Shelby. You already hold down a full-time job and have Ryan to care for." He dug through his drawer and pulled out a black T-shirt and handed it to her.

"Thank you." Their eyes met and she didn't move.

Cullen was slowly losing his resolve to maintain his distance. He wanted nothing more than to keep her here with him. If she were right beside him, then he'd know she was safe. "I think you best go to bed. Because in about ten seconds, I'm not going to let you leave here, and you won't be needing that shirt."

THE NEXT MORNING came with bright sunlight coming through the window. Shelby had managed to get up on time. She'd gotten herself up and ready for work, but when she went to get Ryan he was gone.

She panicked until she hurried downstairs and heard laughter coming from the kitchen. That was where she found Ryan with Cullen.

Her nephew saw her first. "Aunt Shellie, you got up. Cullen is taking me to school in his truck."

She noticed that the child had on a clean shirt. "Oh, really? That will be fun." She looked at Cullen and lowered her voice. "You don't have to do that."

"I know. But since you take him in so early, and I don't have to be at the office until eight, it's just easier for all of us."

He looked at Ryan. "Hey, kid, you better go upstairs and brush your teeth. I put a new toothbrush in the bathroom."

"Okay." The boy jumped down and took off upstairs.

Cullen walked to the coffeemaker and poured her a cup, then handed it to her. "I was up feeding the horses, and when I got back I heard Ryan stirring." He shrugged. "Seemed foolish to bother you when he only wanted to eat some cereal."

"Well, thank you," she said. "I can't tell you how much I appreciate what you're doing for us."

He offered her a small smile. "Like I said, our motto is Protect and Serve."

She nodded. "I'll go and check on Ryan to make sure he's ready for school." She paused. "You sure you don't mind taking him?"

"Not at all. In fact, I want to check the security policy at the school." When he saw her panic, he said, "It's just a precaution, Shelby."

She heard Ryan coming down the stairs. "Aunt Shellie." He rushed into the kitchen. "Can I take my picture book to school?"

Georgia had told her that Ryan had trouble getting obsessed with certain things. His picture book was one of them. Yet, those pictures had been a source of comfort over the tragedy of losing his mother. Thank God, the book hadn't been in the cottage last night. "Just for today."

The boy rewarded her with a smile, then retrieved the small album off the table. "Ready, Cullen?"

Shelby wasn't sure what today would bring, but she knew she wasn't alone. Sheriff Cullen was there to help her. For the first time since Georgia's death, she felt she wasn't alone.

Chapter Eleven

Cullen walked into the sheriff's office right before eight that morning. The day shift had just come on duty, and Connie was at her desk, going over the previous night's calls. She looked up and smiled.

"Good morning, Cullen."

He smiled back. She never called him Sheriff. He knew her loyalty was with her brother, Ted. "Good morning, Connie." He stopped in front of the high counter. "Quiet night?"

She nodded. "Yes. Just a few routine traffic stops."

"That's the way I like it." He took the printout from her and went into his office. After closing the glass-paneled door for some privacy, he sat down at his desk.

The place really wasn't his, but he'd cleared out some of Ted's things just to have more room. This community loved Ted Carson, as they should. He'd done an excellent job for a lot of years. Cullen appreciated that kind of dedication.

His attention turned to Shelby and what she'd told him. If someone was following her, he needed to find out who.

He picked up the phone and dialed the Dawkins Meadow Police Department. When the dispatcher answered, the man asked, "How may I direct your call?"

"Captain Kershaw, please. Sheriff Cullen Brannigan. I'm calling from Hidden Springs, Colorado."

Even before he'd decided to make the call, he had done some checking on the small Kentucky town. He'd been up most of the night reading about Georgia Hughes's murder.

"This is Captain Kershaw. What can I do for you, Sheriff?"

"I'm calling about the investigation of Georgia Hughes's murder. I was wondering if you have any leads, or have made any arrests."

There was a long pause, then the captain said, "May I ask why you want to know?"

He might as well lay it out there, praying he wasn't putting his trust in the wrong man. "We have two new residents here, Shelby Townsend and her nephew, Ryan Hughes. They'd appreciate some closure on Georgia."

"I can't divulge anything about an ongoing investigation. All I can tell you is that we're checking all avenues."

Cullen couldn't let it go. "What about Gil Bryant? For a time, he was involved with Mrs. Hughes. From what I heard from her sister, Miss Townsend, Bryant had been threatening her. All three had planned to leave town the night Georgia was killed. Seems to me that would put the man at the top of the suspect list."

"Like I said, this is an ongoing investigation." There was a long pause, then the captain said, "Tell Miss Townsend that we're doing everything possible to bring her sister's killer to justice."

"So you are getting close?"

"Believe me, Sheriff, I want to bring this murder to justice more than you know."

Cullen hoped he wasn't just getting lip service. "Good, then you won't mind me checking back in with you."

LATER IN THE AFTERNOON, Shelby watched out the window as Cullen took Ryan out to the barn to feed the horses. She decided that to thank Cullen for his kindness, she would cook him supper. Besides, the busywork helped distract her. So she worked at putting together ingredients for her homemade lasagna.

Once she placed the pan into the oven, she set the timer. She looked around Cullen's large kitchen, and ideas flooded her head. Wouldn't it be nice to have all this space to work? There were plenty of cabinets for dishes and spices. Okay, maybe the tiled counters needed to be replaced, and maybe a stainless steel island for added room to roll out pie dough.

She shook her head. What was she thinking? This was Cullen's home. She wasn't even sure if she could stay in this town, and let alone in this beautiful house.

Staying in the cottage was close enough to the man. And she needed to move back there and fast. She'd intruded on Cullen's life long enough. Her thoughts went to Gil Bryant. Was she being paranoid? Maybe she had forgotten to close the front door yesterday. They had been in a hurry to get over to Kase and Laurel's house.

At the window she looked out to see that Cullen had placed Ryan on Sassy's bare back and was walking her back to the barn. She smiled, watching the other horses follow the leader. He had a way with animals. She looked at the smiling Ryan. And kids, too.

More and more this man was working his way into her heart, and that scared her. She didn't trust easily, ever since her grandmother's death, then losing Georgia. It was hard to risk her heart again. She thought back to last night. How Cullen had protected her, made her feel safe. A warm tingling swirled low in her stomach.

Whoa. Not good. She didn't want to fall hard for the

sheriff, and have him go back to Denver. She still couldn't help but wonder why he'd left the police department. He had to be good at his job, or he wouldn't have been hired for the sheriff position here.

She shook her head. She didn't need Cullen Brannigan. He'd distracted her too much as it was. She had to keep her focus on her future. Hidden Springs held great possibilities for her. She had a chance to buy into a catering business. Make her own hours so she could be with Ryan, and more important, make a home for both of them.

Suddenly her phone chimed, letting her know she was getting a text. She tensed. Very few people knew her new number. She picked up her phone and looked at the message. It was a picture. Slowly a smile began to spread across her face as she examined the photo of the two brand-new babies. One swaddled in a blue blanket and the other in pink.

"Well, doesn't that beat all. A boy and a girl."

She texted back. Congrats, Mom and Dad. They're precious. She blinked back the tears in her eyes. How wonderful it would be to have a baby. Not now, of course. She had a sweet little boy already, but someday...

She decided to go outside and share the news. Once out the back door, she headed for the corral, where she found the twosome.

Ryan waved. "Aunt Shellie, I'm riding Cloud."

"You sure are, sweetie."

She turned her attention to Cullen. "I just received this message." She handed him the phone.

He frowned and looked at the text, then a big smile appeared across his face. Her heart did a flip.

"Cute." He showed the picture to Ryan and explained, "Those are Addy's new brother and sister."

"Two of them?"

They all laughed, then Ryan sobered and said, "I want a brother, too."

Cullen shot a glance at Shelby.

What was she supposed to say to that? But before she had the chance, Ryan said, "I can't 'cause I don't have a mom and dad." He lowered his head.

Cullen reached up and pulled him down off the horse into his arms. "Hey, don't be sad. You have your Aunt Shellie. And you know she loves you as much as your mom and dad."

The boy nodded, then slowly his face brightened. "And someday she will have a baby, too."

"That could happen." Cullen stole a glance at her. His heated gaze locked on hers. She felt such a jolt through her body she had to look away.

"But for now, buddy, you're her little boy."

Cullen went on to say, "And what a lucky kid. You get to eat all her delicious cakes and cookies."

Ryan rewarded him with a smile. "Yeah, I do."

Cullen winked at Shelby, then set the boy down. "Now, why don't you run up to the house and wash up?"

Ryan went to his aunt and hugged her. "I love you, Aunt Shellie."

She hugged him back, fighting tears. "I love you, too, Ryan."

He released her. "Can I play with my tablet?"

"Yes, until I get there."

When the child ran toward the back door, Shelby turned back to Cullen. "Thank you. I never heard him say anything like that before."

Cullen shrugged. He probably should have stayed out of her personal life, but since that first night he hadn't been able to manage to do that. "Kids are bound to have questions. Both Ryan's parents are gone. He wants a family like everyone else." He smiled, remembering his own childhood. "When Leslie married Dad and moved in, I was older than Ryan at ten years old, but I wondered if there would be more kids, too."

"Should I worry about this?"

Cullen shrugged. "Ryan just wants what Addy has. Right now that's a horse, and siblings. He gets to ride a horse, and he has love and stability."

"The love part is easy, but stability, I'm not sure."

"And you're doing a terrific job with him."

"Thank you. Loving Ryan is easy."

He looked into her eyes. Damn, if she didn't get him all stirred up. "I'm only speaking the truth."

The word *truth* caused Cullen to pause and recall his earlier conversation with the police captain. He quickly decided to hold off until there was more information. Besides, he liked seeing her carefree mood.

Shelby pointed toward the house. "I put lasagna in the oven. It should be ready in an hour or so." She hesitated, then said, "Thank you for letting us stay last night. I'll get Ryan and head back to the cottage."

When she turned to leave, he couldn't help but stop her when he captured her by the arm. "No, you can't leave. I can't possibly eat all that lasagna by myself. You and Ryan need to help me."

She looked up at him with those incredible blue eyes. "I shouldn't. We intruded so much already."

He took a step closer. "Have you heard me complain?"

She smiled. "No, but…"

He leaned down, closer to her so he could inhale her clean, lemony scent. "What do I need to do to convince you to stay?"

She looked him in the eyes. "Oh, Cullen. You don't

need to convince me. You've been so generous…letting us intrude in your home."

He didn't feel he was the one who was generous. He'd been living in the big house, alone. She and Ryan breathed life back into the faded walls. "You're not intruding. You cooked the meal, so please stay and have supper with me?"

AFTER SUPPER, CULLEN played a video game with Ryan on his large television. That was until he discovered the boy had crashed. He wanted to carry the child upstairs and put him to bed where he knew if there was a bad guy, he could protect them. Of course, Aunt Shellie wouldn't put up with him taking away her independence.

Cullen glanced down at the boy sagged against his side, sound asleep. He shut off the game, and got up slowly so as not to disturb him, then laid Ryan down on the sofa. He covered him with a blanket and went in search of Shelby in the kitchen.

He stopped in the doorway and watched her washing up the last of the dishes. He couldn't help but appreciate the woman's nice curves, her small waist, her round, firm bottom and long legs. Yet, he found being with Shelby was more than just a carnal response. He just plain liked spending time with her. But for how much longer would she be around if there was a crazed cop scaring her out of town? If only for her protection, he needed to convince her to stay.

"You don't have to wash those," he told her.

Shelby gasped and turned around. "If you keep sneaking up on me, I'll quit and leave the dirty pots and pans."

"Then do it." He went to her and took her hand. "Come with me. We need to talk."

"What about Ryan?"

"At the moment, he's asleep. So that gives us a chance to discuss a few things."

After proof that her nephew was asleep, she let him lead her into an office under the stairs. The wood paneling was dark and a little dingy, and so were the cream-colored walls. There was a big oak desk against one wall. He'd brought a few of his things in here, including a fax machine and his laptop computer.

He directed her to the camel-colored leather love seat against the wall. "You found out something about Gil, didn't you?"

He hesitated, then knew he couldn't keep the information from her. He picked up the folder on the desk and handed it to her.

"Yes, I checked out Gil Bryant. His file states he's not your ideal cop. He's been charged with assault and battery, but the charges were dropped, twice. The guy had a problem with drinking, too, but he went through alcohol rehab and was reinstated on the force." Cullen sighed. "It's not a glowing report. In fact, I'm surprised that when your sister made the original complaint, they didn't believe her."

"Georgia was afraid to take it too far. Afraid Gil would retaliate. He did. He hounded her, followed her, then he killed her." He saw her frustration. "I just wished we could have proved it."

"I don't want you to be involved in any way with this man, Shelby. He's dangerous."

"But if Georgia had proof…"

"We'll find it, but together. Then I can talk to someone I can trust."

Her eyes widened. "You know someone, don't you?"

"Yes, I talked with Captain Kershaw this morning."

She paused. "What did he tell you?"

"Mainly that Georgia's death is still an open investigation, but he's directing all his attention toward Bryant. He's learned more information about a drug operation in town." He shook his head. "I've said too much."

He sat down beside Shelby. "This might take some time, Shelby, but they'll get this guy. And if it is Gil, and he's found you here, then he's pretty desperate. Maybe because the guys he works for are after him to take care of loose ends. I need to protect you and Ryan."

She nodded, then raised her sock-covered feet onto the sofa and rested her head on her knee. "I'm just so tired of being afraid, of looking over my shoulder."

Cullen sat down beside her, wrapped his arms around her and pulled her close. Damn, she felt good. "I know this has been rough on you. You've taken on a lot, and you haven't even had time to mourn the loss of your sister."

She sniffed and raised her head. "All those years apart, then we didn't get much time together."

Cullen's heart was breaking for her. "You said when your grandmother died you'd been separated."

Shelby nodded.

He couldn't hide his surprise. "I didn't think they split up siblings anymore."

"Sometimes there isn't a choice. In our case, I was young enough to go into a private home, but they didn't want two foster kids. So Georgia stayed in a group home." She waved it off. "It was a long time ago. All that matters now is for me to raise Ryan."

"We're going to do everything we can to keep him safe."

"No, Cullen. You can't spend all day and night worrying about us. You have a job to do."

"And I'm doing that job." He glanced away, then back at her. "Okay, it's a temporary job, but that doesn't mean I'll shirk any of my duties while I'm here in town."

"Then you're going back to Denver?"

He shook his head. "No. I told you my career there is over."

She studied him for a moment. "Why is it over, Cullen?"

He hesitated.

"Come on, Sheriff, you know everything about me. Let me get a peek at your past."

He leaned forward and placed his elbows on his knees. "I was a detective on the white-collar crime task force. A year ago, I was on an undercover operation when I was indicted for internet fraud and for taking bribes."

He heard her gasp but continued, "I was set up when someone leaked that I was law enforcement. As it turned out, it was my former partner. Since we were friends, he had access to my apartment and could get my bank account information and insert the payments. I looked guilty. It took nearly a year to clear my name and get re-instated on the police force."

She shook her head. "Wow! Our stories are so similar."

"Yeah, you're running from a crooked cop, and I've been accused of being one."

He felt her hand on his back, and he turned and looked at her.

"That's where the comparison ends, Cullen. This town would have never hired you if there was any doubt about your innocence."

He nodded, unable to express how much her faith meant to him. He hadn't gotten much of that over the past year.

She leaned forward and wrapped her arms around him. "I'm so sorry, Cullen."

Need shot through him as she spoke his name in a low, husky voice. He sat back and pulled her onto his lap, so he was cradling her close. His hands went to cup her cheeks as his attention zeroed in on her mouth. "It was a long time ago, Shelby. I only want to think about now." His mouth brushed hers, and he heard her quick intake of breath. "And you."

God, he shouldn't be doing this, but he went back for more. He lowered his head once again and his mouth covered hers in a hungry kiss, and she wrapped her arms around his neck, digging her fingers into his scalp. He groaned, then deepened the kiss, brushing his tongue across the seam of her lips. She opened immediately and he dived inside to taste her, but it only fueled his hunger. He tore his mouth away, then pressed kisses all the way up to her ear, feeling her shiver.

"Damn, I want you." He cupped her face as his gaze swept over her azure eyes, the hue deepened with desire, and her full lips. He couldn't get enough, and he lowered his head and kissed her again, and again.

He tore his mouth away, and fought to draw air into his lungs. "We better slow down." This was crazy for him to get involved with her during an investigation.

She glanced away. "You're right." She started to sit up, and he stopped her.

"You think I want to end this? I don't, but if I'm thinking about us, and not who might be out there trying to get to you, I'm not doing my job."

"You're very good at your job, Sheriff." She gave him a coy smile as her arms circled his neck. "But I wouldn't want to distract you from your duty."

"Too late. The second you'd opened the door that first night you got my attention." He lowered his head when there was a knock on the door. "Who the hell is that?" Thinking it could be one of his men, he shifted her off his lap and stood.

"Be right back." He walked out of the office into the

hall. Once he reached the door, he looked through the glass panel to see an older man on the porch. His mood quickly soured. What the hell? He turned the latch and opened the door.

"What are you doing here?"

"Nice welcome." Neal Brannigan pushed past him and walked into the house. "I came to see my son."

Chapter Twelve

Shelby heard arguing in the hall. Who was here? Worried something was wrong, she went to find out.

In the entry was Cullen and a man who could be his twin but was twenty years his senior. The older man had thick gray hair that was cut short. He was tall with a sinewy build, still broad-shouldered and muscular. She had no doubt that the man was Cullen's father.

She started to back away to give them privacy when the man noticed her. She stopped. "Excuse me," she said, getting Cullen's attention.

"Shelby, this is my father, Neal Brannigan. Dad, this is Shelby Townsend."

She went to them. "Hello, Mr. Brannigan, it's nice to meet you."

The man nodded. "It's nice to meet you, too, Miss Townsend." He glanced at his son. "I didn't mean to interrupt."

"You could have called," Cullen said.

"I did call," his father argued. "You just didn't answer."

"Cullen," Shelby said, in a calming voice. "Why don't you take your father into the kitchen and I'll put on some coffee before I take Ryan home?" She pointed to the family room, where the child slept.

"You're right," Cullen said. "Come on, Dad."

Shelby went on ahead and they followed quietly. Once in the kitchen, she put the grounds into the coffeemaker, then took down two mugs. She went to the counter and unwrapped the rest of the caramel cake they had for supper. She put out place mats and took down two plates.

"Mr. Brannigan, how do you like your coffee?"

"Black. And please, call me Neal."

"And I'm Shelby."

He nodded and looked at his son. "What happened to the Donaldsons?"

Cullen leaned against the counter. He didn't want to stand here and go over his decision to rent the cottage. "They moved out right after Trent and I inherited the place. Shelby and Ryan needed a place to live, so she's renting it."

"Do you think that's a good idea, son, to have a single woman out here alone, especially since you're the acting sheriff?"

He shook his head. "Even for you, that's out of line."

Shelby jumped in. "I should get Ryan to bed." She started to leave.

Cullen held up a hand to stop her. "You're not going anywhere, Shelby." He turned to his father. "You can't come in here and make accusations, not when you don't know the situation. But you're good at that, right, Dad?"

The lines on Mr. Brannigan's forehead deepened. "I'm only saying… Okay, I'll mind my own business."

"Yeah, right. That'll be the day."

Shelby walked out of the kitchen, leaving the two men to argue. She gathered Ryan's things and stuffed them into her oversize bag, all the time trying to forget what happened between them in the office. It had been inappropriate.

"Shelby…"

She turned at the sound of Cullen's voice.

"I'm sorry about what my dad said."

"No, he was right, and you were right, too. I shouldn't be here, distracting you from your job."

He took a step closer, and she backed up. "No. What happened in the office was a mistake. You need to think about your future. Neither one of us should do anything foolish right now."

Had she hoped to get an argument? When he didn't say anything, she had her answer. She hooked her purse over her shoulder and went to scoop up Ryan in her arms.

"Let me get him," Cullen said, then called to his dad he'd be right back.

She didn't even dispute him and stood back, allowing him to pick up the child. Ryan stirred, but Cullen soothed him quickly and walked into the kitchen. "Good night, Neal," she called. "It was nice meeting you."

"Same here. Good night."

Once at the cottage, she unlocked the door, but was still feeling a little anxious coming back here. Well, she needed to get over it. At least until she found them another place to live.

Cullen carried Ryan into his bedroom. After Shelby removed his shoes and socks and jeans, she tucked him under the covers. She walked out and closed the door, and he reached for her.

She gasped as she ended up in his arms and his mouth took hers in a fierce kiss. She couldn't stop from reacting, stop wanting him, stop needing him. Finally he released her.

"This isn't over, Shelby." He brushed his mouth over hers again. "You're safe here. I've checked all the locks, but if you need me…for anything, call. Good night." He turned and walked out, before she could even find the breath to speak.

On the way back to the house, Cullen worked to cool down. His father appearing at his door still had him riled, but he couldn't keep running away. It was time to face the man and stand up to whatever he had to dish out. He opened the back door and found his father seated at the table.

He was eating cake. "I'll say one thing, your Shelby sure can bake."

"That's because she's a chef." He went to pour himself a cup of coffee. "If you're hungry there's leftover lasagna in the fridge."

"This will hold me until morning." He took another bite. "How long have you known her?"

"About a month when she came here for a job. Like I said, she and her nephew are renting the cottage."

Even knowing that the coffee would keep him awake, Cullen filled his mug. He doubted his father was leaving for a while. He took a sip. "Why are you here, Dad?"

"I didn't like how we left things."

The last thing he wanted was to rehash the past. "And whose fault is that?"

"It's mine," his father admitted. "I should have handled your suspension differently."

"My suspension? You mean my indictment?"

Neal raised a hand. "Okay, I was wrong. I should have stood by you. Is that what you want me to say?"

"I want you to tell me the truth. Did you really think I was guilty?"

Without any hesitation, Neal shook his head. "No, but everything's political these days. I was told by my superiors to stay out of the mix, that there was a bigger investigation going on." He leaned forward. "I had to keep my distance, son. As you know, there were several men in the department under suspicion. I was told to not take sides because they were trying to find out who else was involved." His father's pain was so obvious. "Leslie kept me filled in on what was going on. I knew she was there for you because I couldn't be."

Cullen's anger softened, seeing the sadness at the mention of his deceased wife's name. "So you're saying, you believed me."

He nodded. "I was never happy about your decision to go undercover. Especially since your partner, Ben Crammer, was a loser, but you were protective of him."

"So I was a slow learner." He hated that he'd been so foolish. "It won't happen again."

His father eyed him closely. "Now that that's settled, don't you think you've had enough time off? You've been reinstated, Cullen, so go get your job back. You could have your pick of any department you want, even have a pension."

The man hadn't been listening. "I'm not going back, Dad."

His father pushed his plate away. "Why the hell not? And don't say it's because no one believed you. That's in the past. Now that you've been proven innocent, there won't be any questions."

"Look, Dad. I had a couple of grueling years. After my undercover work and the year on trial, I need some time to think about what I want. Captain Brewer gave me a year to decide to come back or not."

"Are you saying you'd rather be a small-town sheriff?"

"Yes, for now. Besides, I signed a contract with the sheriff's department, at least for the next few months."

"I can't believe you're giving up everything you've worked for."

"Yes, I worked hard for over ten years. I still have partial retirement and back-pay settlement. And now, I'm part owner in this ranch."

Neal released a long sigh. "I guess I'll never understand this. You love being in law enforcement."

"And I am in law enforcement. I don't have to go back to a large city to find work." He straightened. "Look, we're not going to agree on this, not tonight anyway. And I have the early shift tomorrow, so I need some sleep."

"Fine. You going to kick your dad out, or you going to let me bunk here?"

Cullen eyed him closely. "You want to stay out here? What about your job?"

Neal smiled. "I guess I forgot to mention, as of last week I'm retired. Like you, I can do what I please. So can you put up with me for a few weeks?"

This time Cullen did groan. What was he going to do now? "There's a bed upstairs, second door on the left. I'll get some sheets for you."

"Thanks, son."

"Like you gave me a choice. Just be assured you aren't the only boarder I have staying here. There'll be four equines up bright and early, ready to be fed."

THE NEXT MORNING, Shelby had Ryan already in the car to leave for work when she noticed Neal Brannigan's truck parked in the drive. Maybe father and son had worked out some issues. She started the engine and drove past the barn.

"Look, Aunt Shellie." She heard the panic in Ryan's voice. "A man."

Neal Brannigan came out of the corral gate. "That's Cullen's father, Mr. Brannigan."

She rolled down the window and called out, "Good morning, Neal."

The man looked so serious. "Morning to you, Shelby." He walked up to the car and bent down to see inside, then his demeanor changed at seeing Ryan. "Well, hello, young man, what is your name?"

"Ryan," he said shyly.

"Well, that's a nice name."

"Did you feed the horses?" Ryan asked.

"Sure did. And they were hungry, too. Do you ride?"

Ryan nodded. "Cullen teaches me."

"Good. Now I better let you go so you can get to school." He stepped back and waved them off.

Shelby drove away and wondered how long Neal Brannigan was staying. She smiled, knowing with his being here, she could focus on her life, and Cullen could focus on his. So why wasn't she happy?

By the time she arrived at work, she quickly started her prep for the morning rush. She kept her eye on the clock, knowing she needed to run Ryan over to school soon.

She heard a knock on the screen door off the alley, and she looked to see Cullen. He smiled, and her heart started to race. "I hear someone here needs a ride to school."

"Cullen, that's not necessary."

Suddenly a smiling Bess came through the restaurant door. "Hello, Sheriff."

"Hi, Bess."

"Come by for breakfast?"

"No, I thought since I had a few minutes before my shift starts, I'd run Ryan to school so Shelby didn't have to stop what she was doing."

The child ran to him. "Cullen."

Shelby wiped her hands on a towel, to distract herself

from drooling over the man in his uniform. "You really don't have to keep taking him, Cullen."

"I know." He arched an eyebrow as Bess wandered off to the other side of the kitchen. "Unless you have a problem with me taking him."

"Of course not." She glanced at Ryan. "I just didn't want you to go to any trouble."

"No trouble. Trouble is my father moving into my house."

She smiled. "We saw Neal this morning. I see you put him to work."

"Yeah, he might as well stay busy. Says he's retired now." He sighed. "That surprised me the most. I thought the man wouldn't leave until they threw him out the door."

She smiled. "Maybe it's good for you to spend some time together and get things straightened out between you."

Cullen sighed. "I'm not so sure. Hey, would you like to come to supper tonight?"

She could tell he was asking for her help. "I think you mean, would you cook supper tonight?"

"You'd really help a lot if you and Ryan could be there so we're not just staring at each other."

"What would you like me to cook?"

"Anything simple. Text me a list of groceries you'll need and I'll buy them."

"Good idea." She kissed Ryan goodbye and grabbed his backpack. She waved as they drove off.

When she came back inside, Bess said, "I'd say you got yourself a nice man there."

"I can't get involved with him, Bess."

"Honey, don't look now, but you're already involved. So start enjoying it."

CULLEN LEANED AGAINST the railing and watched his father lead Ryan around the corral on Cloud. Tightness banded his chest as he remembered how the man used to do the same with him and Austin. They couldn't have been more than Ryan's age when they'd learned to ride.

Then his father's first wife, Cullen and Austin's mother, Mary, died. His dad never recovered from the loss. A widower for three years, he met and married Leslie Landry, but he still wasn't the man he once was. Detective Neal Brannigan worked more on criminal cases and stayed at the office and away from home.

Cullen never understood how Leslie had been able to put up with a marriage where she was alone all the time. He smiled recalling his loving stepmother. How she'd always show up to all his and Austin's ball games and school events. Dad always had an excuse not to be there, always had something to do with work.

Maybe that had been why Cullen had gone into police work. To impress his father. To get his attention. Yet, years later all his commendations and successes with the force had never earned him any praise. Then the indictment came down, and he'd hoped his father would at least stand up for him. It didn't happen, either. He had to deal with the fact that nothing he did would please the man.

"They both seem to be having fun."

He tensed, then realized Shelby had come up behind him. He climbed off the railing. "Yeah, it's hard to tell who's having the most fun."

Shelby looked through the fence slats and waved at Ryan. "How long is your father staying?"

He shrugged. "Your guess is as good as mine."

She nodded. "With the recent death of his wife, he probably needs you and your brother."

"Well, he had a lot of years to spend time with us, and

he never seemed to want to. So I doubt this visit will be a long one."

Shelby was quiet for a moment, then said, "As a person who's had little family, take the time to be with him." She turned back toward the action in the corral. "I can't even remember my parents. Well, I never did meet my father, and my mother died in a car accident when I was six. Grandma Ivy was my and Georgia's lifeline. I have wonderful memories of her," she said, her voice husky with emotion. "Sometimes that just isn't enough, and you get so lonely your insides ache."

Cullen found himself reaching out and wrapping his arms around her. "Hey, Shelby, don't. I'm sorry you lost them." He cradled her close, feeling her tremble. "You are so lucky to have Ryan." He pulled back and looked into her eyes. "The boy adores you. I'd say you're doing a wonderful job with him."

She smiled. "Thank you."

"Hey, you two!"

Cullen heard the familiar voice and turned around to see Trent. He immediately stepped back from Shelby. "Hey there, bro. What brings you out here?" He glanced toward the truck. "Another horse?"

Trent smiled. "No. No more horses at the moment. Hi, Shelby."

"Hi, Trent. How are your new niece and nephew doing?"

He shook his head in disbelief. "They're incredible. Little Jackson Rory, called 'Jack,' and Caitlin Diane, 'Katy' for short, are doing great. Better than their exhausted parents."

Shelby couldn't hide her excitement. "I'd love to go see them, but I know they don't need any visitors right now. Maybe I'll cook a meal and run it by tomorrow after work."

"They'd appreciate that, I'm sure," Trent said. "Brooke is over there right now to help out."

Cullen knew Trent didn't just come by to shoot the breeze. "So what else brings you by?"

"I got that therapy saddle."

"Really?" Shelby said.

Trent nodded. "Alice Bradley was happy to donate it to the cause. It's in the truck." He looked back at Cullen. "I also got a call from Neal. Said he was in town and wanted to see me. Do you have any idea what it's about?"

Cullen shook his head. "No. He showed up last night. Told me he retired from the force and wanted to visit a few days."

Trent frowned. "Well, the two of us never really bonded all those years ago, or again at Mom's funeral, so I can't imagine why he wants to see me. If it's to dispute her will—"

"No, I don't think it's that," Cullen disagreed. "Before they got married, I overheard them discussing how to separate their finances."

Trent nodded, then they all turned toward the corral and the man leading Ryan on the horse.

"Maybe he's just lonely," Shelby suggested. "He and Ryan seem to be getting along."

The older man looked over at them and waved. "Hey, Trent." Neal Brannigan smiled. "It's good to see you." He tugged on the lead rope to walk the horse closer. Trent opened the gate, and all three of them stepped inside.

"Hi, Ryan."

The boy grinned. "Hi, Trent."

Trent looked at his stepfather. "How have you been, Neal?"

The older man tipped his hat back. "Not too bad. I miss your mother."

Cullen saw Trent tense. "We all do."

Neal nodded. "I brought some of her personal things, mostly pictures. I thought you might like to have them."

Trent nodded. "I appreciate that."

Shelby stepped in. "Trent, since Brooke is helping Laurel with the twins, why don't you stay for supper? It's only meat loaf and garlic mashed potatoes, but I made pineapple cake for dessert."

Trent smiled. "I guess I can stay."

Ryan's grin broadened. "Oh, boy."

"Help me with the horses, Trent," Cullen said.

"So I got to work for my meal?"

"Hey, I seem to remember, you were the one who brought those animals here."

Neal smiled. "Brings back memories."

Cullen took the gelding from his father. He hoped that tonight's family supper was going to be filled with a few good memories for a change.

Chapter Thirteen

Later that evening, thunder rumbled through the big house. Shelby felt Ryan jump, but the tense mood at the supper table had nothing to do with the spring storm. She glanced around the kitchen table at the three men. They looked as awkward as if they were all strangers, not family. Even the meal she'd worked so hard on was being ignored.

The scene was painful to watch. So she tried to ease the tension. "So, Neal, do you have any plans now that you're retired? Travel, maybe?"

He looked at her and smiled. "I might travel some. I thought I'd catch a few rodeos."

That got Cullen's attention. "You're going to go see Austin?"

Neal gave a nod. "Thought I might." He looked at Cullen. "Maybe you'd like to go along."

Shelby held her breath, waiting to hear the answer.

"Now's not a good time."

"Well, I could wait until you're finished with your job here."

Cullen pushed his food around on his plate. "We'll see."

Shelby sat back, listening to the sound of the rain on the roof and the distant thunder. At least one storm was moving on.

Trent drew her attention. "Shelby, I'm not sure if you know that Rory and I own hunting and fishing cabins, and also the Q and L Guest Lodge, which we rent out for weddings and parties. We've always used All Occasions Catering, but Bess said we should talk with you. Have you taken over the business?"

"Not exactly, but I am handling most of the catering. Bill and Bess need some free time." She wondered if she'd taken on too much.

Trent arched an eyebrow. "So you're staying here?"

She'd love to if Gil stayed out of her life, and if someone else cared enough. She gave a quick glance at Cullen, who was talking to his dad. "We'll see how things work out."

"I hope you stay in our town," Trent said. "I know Laurel and Brooke would love having another woman close by."

"I wish I had more time to spend with friends. Working full time, it's been difficult."

"Do you feel isolated out here?"

She felt Cullen's gaze. "Oh, no. Of course, it's a little longer drive to town, but I love living in the country. It reminds me of my childhood on the farm."

Trent rested his arms on the table. "The reason for asking about the catering business was because Rory and I are building more cabins on the property. It seems our weddings are so popular that the families and friends want to stay on the property. So we're wondering if you'd be interested in doing a Sunday brunch." He raised a hand. "Before you answer, we have a full-service kitchen in the lodge, so you could keep all the supplies on-site and not have to bring them in each week. And of course we're only open in spring and summer."

"Wow, you really are expanding your business."

"These days we can't just rely on cattle to make a living." Trent Landry's grin was contagious and his brown eyes were captivating. "I've sampled your incredible cooking skills, Shelby, but I have a feeling we've only tapped into your talents."

"Thank you. It's nice to know that I'm so popular."

"I think you knew that when you started working for the café," Trent said. "Just think about the brunch."

She nodded, then felt a tug on her sleeve. "I ate all my vegetables," Ryan said. "Can I have dessert?"

"Yes, you may," she told him and stood. "Gentlemen, would you all like coffee with dessert?"

Cullen got up, too. "I'll get the coffee." He went to the cupboard and took down the mugs while she went to the cake on the counter. She cut sizable slices and placed them on dessert plates. She brought them to the table, and the men eagerly dug in.

Trent was the first one to speak. "You'll have to give this recipe to Brooke."

Ryan looked up and grinned, cake crumbs around his mouth. "It's good, Aunt Shellie."

The men laughed, and surprisingly it was Neal who reached over and wiped the boy's mouth on the napkin. "There you go, son."

"Thanks," Ryan said. "Pops."

Shelby froze. Oh, my, where had Ryan decided on that name?

Neal looked at her. "I hope you don't mind that I told Ryan he could call me Pops. It's a nickname I inherited from the young guys on the force."

She shook her head. "No, not as long as you gave him permission."

Neal nodded. "He's been very respectful. And he's learning to ride pretty quick, too."

Ryan smiled. "I want to go riding again. Can Noah come, too?"

She looked at Cullen, who seemed to be ignoring her most of the meal. "We'll have to see."

Neal spoke up. "I could take him."

Cullen sat back in his chair. What was his father doing? Since when had the man turned so domestic? "There's no need, Dad." He looked at the boy. "We can go after work tomorrow."

That brought a big grin from Ryan, and his chest swelled a little.

Cullen turned to Trent. "I'm off about noon tomorrow, and if you have time I thought we could start on the ramp."

Trent nodded. "Yeah, I could come for a few hours. What about you, Neal? You want to help, too?"

Cullen wasn't sure if he needed his father critiquing his work. But what the hell. "Yeah, Dad, you want to help?"

"Sure."

"Since you have the therapy saddle," Shelby began, "do you want me to mention the idea to Jeanie?"

Cullen nodded. "I guess you should. If his parents don't want their son to ride, we need to know."

"The ramp is a good idea, even if we only use it so the kids can learn to mount." Trent pushed his chair from the table and stood. "Well, I need to go and pick up Chris and Brooke at Laurel's. Thanks for supper, bro. Shelby, it was delicious."

Shelby stood, too. "Tell Laurel I'll stop by tomorrow to drop off some food."

"I'll let her know." Trent surprised her when he embraced her in a hug.

"Anytime," she said. "And give those babies a kiss for me."

"Good night, Neal, Cullen." He ruffled Ryan's hair. "Night, kid."

Trent shook Neal's hand and picked up the box of pictures the older man had given him earlier, then he and Cullen headed for the back door. Once outside in the cool air, Cullen asked, "Do you have any idea what Dad's up to?"

Trent shook his head. "Neal has never been one of my favorite people. Sorry, but I hated the way he treated my mother."

"I agree. Leslie deserved more from her husband. We deserved more of him, too. That's what surprised me when he showed up yesterday."

"Could be the old guy is lonely. Maybe he realizes what he's been missing with his family all these years."

Cullen knew his dad was a hard man, and he wouldn't make excuses for the man. He wanted to remember Neal Brannigan as he had been before Cullen's mother died. He caught a glimpse of that man with Ryan. He just hoped it lasted.

THE NEXT AFTERNOON, work had begun on the ramp. The wood from the lumberyard had been moved off the truck, and Cullen got busy measuring and cutting the two-by-fours. He stood back as his dad ripped the tongue-and-groove boards with a power saw. Then Trent carried them over to the frame, picked up the nail gun and began placing them along the ramp's incline.

Then Cullen began to measure for the railing. They needed at least one on the side to brace the wheelchair. After a lengthy discussion, they decided the best place for the structure was outside of the corral close to the side gate.

Engrossed in his work, Cullen hadn't heard the approaching car. It wasn't until Ryan appeared beside him that he realized the time.

"How does it look?" he asked.

A big grin appeared on the boy's face. "Good."

The two exchanged a high five. "So will this work for Luke?"

The boy nodded. "Can he ride now?"

Cullen quickly got distracted when he saw Shelby walking toward them. He took notice as she smiled at him, and he felt a hard tug on his body. Realizing he was staring, he turned back to Ryan as he removed his safety glasses. "We'll see."

Shelby smiled, her gaze traveling over their handiwork. "Wow, you guys have been busy. This looks great."

Cullen nodded. "Yeah, Dad found dimensions for building a wheelchair ramp on the internet and Trent brought over lumber from his building site along with some power tools."

His stepbrother stopped nailing the boards and stood. He came over to join them. "So you like our handiwork?"

"You guys amaze me by what you've accomplished in such a short time."

Trent grinned. "It's all my military training. I know how to motivate the troops."

Cullen spoke up. "Yeah, right. You mean you boss everyone around."

Trent surprised him by wrapping his arm around his neck in a choke hold. Years ago, Trent would do this to show his dominance. No more. Cullen quickly got out of the lock, reversed the advantage and whipped his stepbrother's arm around his back.

Just then Neal came out of the barn. "Hey, you two, knock it off."

Cullen quickly released Trent and they both started laughing.

Trent said, "Hey, you've gained some quickness over the years." He eyed Shelby. "Maybe if Brooke was here cheering for me, I might have tried harder."

"Right. And maybe I got the advantage because you aren't bigger than I am any longer."

Shelby watched the two brothers. They were nearly the same size. Trent might be an inch taller, but their muscle mass was pretty much the same. "Hey, boys." She got their attention and nodded toward Ryan. "Some people might not know you're just kidding around."

Cullen's movement was quick as he swooped Ryan up in his arms. "Do you want to play, too?" Soon her nephew was sitting on those broad shoulders and they were chasing Trent around the yard. Ryan was giggling so hard. His happiness brought tears to her eyes.

Soon Neal came out of the barn leading Cloud, saddled and ready to ride. He walked over to them. "I know the railing isn't up yet, but I thought Ryan could try out the ramp."

The guys looked at her. Shelby found she was excited for Ryan to try it, too. "Sure."

Neal led the horse over to the ramp, and everyone else followed with an excited little boy. Cullen took the time to explain the reason for the location. "We placed the ramp close to the corral gate. Also, it's out of the way, and Jeanie can park her van closer." He pointed at the area just past the driveway. Cullen turned to her. "Did you talk with Luke's mother?"

"Yes. She was excited about the idea, but wants to discuss it with her husband."

"That's understandable," Cullen said. "We're probably overstepping to go ahead and do this, huh?"

She didn't agree with that. "I'd say you guys are pretty special to go to all this trouble so a little boy could have a chance to ride."

Cullen shrugged. "I always enjoyed working with kids. I discovered after being a cop, doing things like this is the best kind of downtime."

She nodded. "I can understand that."

Ryan tugged on her hand. "C'mon, Aunt Shellie."

She loved his excitement. "Okay, let's go."

With Cullen right behind them, the child hurried up the new ramp to the platform. Cloud was waiting for him. Neal held on to the bridle as Cullen instructed Ryan on how to mount by himself. Trent was standing on the other side in case something went wrong.

Cullen knelt down beside the boy. "You can do this, Ryan," he coaxed and guided his small foot into the stirrup. "Now reach for the horn and pull up. That's it. Now swing your leg over."

Ryan worked at the task, but struggled until Cullen gave the child's rump a little nudge upward. Once in the saddle, Ryan pumped his fist in the air. "I did it."

Neal began to walk the horse toward the corral to begin the trip around the arena. "He's going to be riding on his own before long," Cullen told her. "Are you ready for that, Aunt Shellie?"

"I'm never ready, but I was riding by myself at his age." She looked up at Cullen. "It's hard being responsible for a child."

"You became an instant mother just a few months ago." His hazel gaze locked on hers. "You're doing great. I just wish you had more free time, not only to spend with him…but with me."

She was taken aback. What did he mean by that? Did he want to date? A relationship? Important question was, did she want to take the chance?

AFTER CLOUD WAS back in the barn, his dad brought in the other horses from the pasture and fed them. Trent took off for home. Neal had Ryan with him and was finishing some things up in the barn. The two seemed to have bonded in a short time. It was odd Neal Brannigan was so attentive, but Cullen wasn't going to question it.

He followed Shelby toward the house, but she started off toward the cottage. Funny, they'd been spending so much time together, it seemed strange to not have her and Ryan with him.

He called to her and she turned around. He caught up to her. "Since you've been cooking so much for me in the past week, I wonder if you'd like to go out to dinner for a change." Damn, if he didn't sound like an awkward teenager. "Nothing fancy, but I know this great hamburger place in town."

She seemed at a loss for words. "I don't know. Maybe Ryan should get an early bedtime."

He caught his father coming out of the barn with Ryan and got an idea. "Hold on a minute." He rushed off to his dad. "Will you do me a favor, and watch Ryan tonight?"

Neal beamed. "Wouldn't mind at all." He looked down at the boy. "How would you like to hang out with me tonight, bud?"

Ryan's blue eyes lit up. "Can we play video games?"

"Sure." Neal looked at Cullen. "Do you have any appropriate games for a five-year-old?"

"Of course." Then Cullen decided he might need to purchase a few more for the future.

Neal smiled. "Okay, we'll hang out together."

Cullen went back to Shelby, Neal and Ryan close behind. "Looks like we have a babysitter for the evening, so Ryan can be in bed early." He smiled. "If it's okay with you that Dad watches him?"

She looked surprised at his suggestion, then she glanced at her nephew. "If Ryan doesn't have a problem, I don't, either."

"Good. And since it's only us, how about we go to a grown-up restaurant? There's a steak house just out of town on the highway."

"You mean the Cliff's Edge Steakhouse?"

He nodded. "What do you do, check out all the competition?"

"No, when I stopped by with some food to see the twins today, Laurel told me about it. That was where Kase promised to take her as soon as the babies can be left with a sitter. I hear the food is very good."

"So you'll go?"

"You mean go…like a real date?"

This was his chance to keep a distance. He couldn't help it, he wanted more time with Shelby. "Yeah, like a real date."

Two hours later, they walked into the steak house. The rustic decor was casual, but nice enough to impress with the rough beams and high ceilings. He went to the hostess station and told her his name. The young girl smiled, picked up two menus and said, "Follow me, Sheriff."

She led them across the carpeted floor, where a big river rock fireplace took up most of one wall. The sun was just descending behind the mountain peak as they sat down at a table in front of the picture window.

She gasped. "Oh, this is an incredible view."

It was pretty close to perfect because she was here. "I

hope the food is as good as the view." He grinned. "It's a challenge to take a chef out to dinner."

"So you've done this before?"

"What, eaten at a steak house, or dated a chef? It's yes and no."

She smiled, and her striking blue eyes were mesmerizing. She wore her rich brown hair down against her shoulders. She had on black trousers and a pretty blue sweater that showed off her trim figure.

She frowned and leaned forward. "Is there something wrong?"

"No, you just look so pretty."

A blush covered her cheeks. "Thank you."

Suddenly he realized how long it had been since he'd been on a date, or even given a woman a compliment. He took her hand. "I'm glad you came with me tonight."

He saw her hesitation, but then she said, "So am I."

The waitress came to the table. "Good evening, I'm Tracy. Is there anything I can get you from the bar?"

They both ordered nonalcoholic beverages, and the waitress walked away. Cullen leaned forward. "You could have ordered something. I just don't want to drink in case I'm called in."

She shook her head. "I'm not much of a drinker, either. Maybe it's because my mother had alcohol and drug issues. And I have a child now to think about."

He nodded in agreement as his fingers wove between her slender ones. He got a rush just holding her hand. "It's instant responsibility, but there are so many bonuses, too. Ryan's a great kid."

"I hope your dad is okay with him tonight."

"The man handled twin sons. I think he can deal with Ryan." He grew serious. "And I get to spend some time with you...alone."

She lowered her eyes coyly, and said, "As my grand-mother would say, 'Are you trying to say you want to court me, Mr. Brannigan?'"

And a helluva lot more. "Yes, I do."

"Even knowing our situation is temporary?"

He squeezed her hand. "Maybe that's a good reason we shouldn't waste any time."

Their beverages arrived, and the waitress discreetly went away.

"That sounds good, except that I have to be worried about Ryan."

"I'm already connected to the boy, and to his aunt. So whether we take this a step further is up to you." He leaned closer to her. "No matter what you decide, Shelby, it won't change our…friendship." Now that the sun had gone down, the candlelight enhanced her beauty. He couldn't help but desire her. What scared him was his feelings going deeper.

"I don't know," she said. "A girl could get hurt." She lowered her long lashes. "What if she comes to care for the guy?"

He decided to put himself out there. "And what if the guy already cares about the girl?"

Chapter Fourteen

Later that night, on the drive back to the ranch, Shelby leaned back against the headrest and closed her eyes. Even though she hadn't had anything to drink, she felt a little light-headed, and nervous about what would happen when they got home.

Neal had called, stating that Ryan had been bathed and he was taking the child to the cottage so he could sleep in his own bed.

Not good. She'd hoped to have the distraction of caring for her nephew to help break the intimacy that had been building between her and Cullen all evening. With Ryan tucked securely in bed, she couldn't help but think about what might happen once they were alone at the cottage.

She glanced across the bench seat at her handsome date, and her heart sped up. She turned her attention back to the road. She had to. She'd never believed in casual sex, and tonight wasn't the time to start.

She tensed as Cullen reached for her hand and placed it on his thigh. Every cell in her body suddenly came alive. Oh, dear. How could she keep resisting the man when back at the restaurant he'd admitted he cared about her?

And, yes, she cared about him, too, but it wasn't just the two of them. There was Ryan to consider in all this.

Yet, with Cullen's hand caressing hers, she wondered if she could stop this fast-moving train.

A crazy thought. Maybe she didn't want to.

Cullen pulled into the drive beside the house.

He raised her hand to his lips and kissed it. "Are you asleep?"

She shivered. "No, just relaxed." She raised her head. "Thank you for a lovely evening."

He leaned closer. "No, thank you." He brushed his mouth across hers, once, twice and a third time. He was a big tease. She wanted more, so much more.

Cullen pulled back. "Maybe we should relieve Dad of babysitting duty. But this first." His head descended toward hers, and this time she wasn't disappointed. He claimed her mouth with a hunger that had her aching to get closer. He hauled her fully against him and she surrendered to him, and opened for him to deepen the kiss. He was like fire burning in her soul.

He tore his mouth away. "After a kiss like that, I might have to wait a minute before I go face my father."

They both laughed, then Cullen got out and walked around to open her door. He lifted her out, but held her close so her body slid down the front of his. With a groan, he took her mouth again and pinned her against the truck as desire nearly swept her away.

With a groan of frustration, he grabbed her hand and walked her to the cottage. Inside they found Neal on the sofa watching television.

Smiling, he stood. "You're home early."

"I have to work in the morning," Shelby said. "How was Ryan?"

"He was great. We played video games for an hour, then came back here and he took a bath, then we watched one of his movies, *Toy Story*."

She went and hugged the man. "Thank you, Neal. I know Ryan enjoyed himself." She glanced at Cullen. "It's just sometimes he has nightmares about his mother."

Neal sobered. "Cullen explained about your sister. I'm sorry for your loss." A smile brightened the older man's face. "Maybe the horseback riding will help him with his sadness."

She was beginning to realize that Ryan was getting attached to so many people here. She didn't want to think about having to leave. "You help, too, Neal. Thank you."

He nodded. "Well, I'm headed back to the house. Good night." He walked out the door and quickly closed it.

Shelby wasn't sure what to do next. She couldn't look Cullen in the eye. The last thing she wanted was for him to see her vulnerability when it came to him. "I should go and check on Ryan," she announced and quickly raced down the hall.

Inside the bedroom, she covered the small child in the bed. He probably had a great time with Neal… Pops. She smiled at the nickname. With a kiss on his forehead, she left the room. She'd just shut the door when she felt Cullen's arms slip around her waist.

Unable to resist, she leaned back against his broad chest, giving him access to her neck, and he took advantage. His lips moved along her sensitive skin, causing the most wonderful shivers.

"Cullen…" she breathed. "What you do to me."

He turned her in his arms, and kissed her again and again. "I know I should leave, but you are making it so damn difficult."

She couldn't speak, mostly afraid of what she'd admit. Instead, her arms circled his neck as his hands tugged her sweater from her waist and slipped underneath to touch her bare skin. She shivered again.

"I want you, Shelby," he breathed. He pulled back and his gaze met hers in the dim light. "It's been a long time since I've let myself care about someone."

She loved hearing his words. "Oh, Cullen…we shouldn't get involved."

His ragged breathing caressed her cheek. "Darlin', we're already involved."

Darn the man for being right. Throwing caution away, she reached up and offered him her mouth. He didn't hesitate and quickly deepened the kiss and began to back her up toward her bedroom. Double darn if she wasn't going willingly. That was until she heard a cell phone ringing.

"Damn." He pulled the phone from his pocket and walked into the living room to talk to the dispatcher.

Reeling from Cullen's kiss, Shelby sagged against the wall. Oh, boy, that was close—too close. Once her legs regained some strength, she made her way into the living room.

He hung up the phone and looked at her. "There's been a bad accident on the highway. I need to go help out."

He came to her, pulled her into his arms and kissed her. When he broke away, he said, "This between us isn't over, Shelby." He kissed her again, then walked out, saying, "Dead-bolt the door."

She called out a good-night, then turned the lock and leaned against the door. She couldn't lock the man out of her heart much longer.

THE NEXT MORNING, Shelby didn't see Cullen's truck when she drove off for work, nor did he show up at the café's back door to take Ryan to school. She was a little concerned, especially after hearing about the pursuit and accident on the highway. And she missed seeing him.

With the breakfast rush over, Shelby took her break

and carried her plate of scrambled eggs, toast and coffee out to the counter. Bill could handle kitchen duties and Bess the cash register while she took a few minutes.

"So you do take a break."

She looked up to see Cullen. Dressed in his sheriff's uniform, he looked official, handsome and tired. "Hi. I've been worried about you. I heard about the crazy man who gave chase last night."

He hung his hat on the coat rack and sat down on the stool beside her. "Yeah, *crazy* explains a lot. Luckily, no one got seriously hurt. But there was a mess of metal slung all over the highway. It took nearly all night to clean up."

"Have you been home?"

Cullen shook his head. He couldn't help but wonder if he hadn't gotten the call if he'd be waking up beside Shelby this morning. Nice dream. "I plan to head there real soon. I have some paperwork to finish up first. That's why I'm here. I need some food to sustain me for a few hours."

"Oh, let me get you something." She started to get up, and he stopped her with his hand on her arm.

"No, you finish your breakfast. Bill can make me some eggs and bacon." Just then the owner walked out of the kitchen and took his order. When Shelby again tried to get up to help, Bill told her to stay and eat.

Cullen looked at Shelby. He was glad that he could steal a few minutes alone with her. "Sorry I wasn't around this morning." He kept his voice low. His gaze met her pretty blue eyes. "The main reason I came was I wanted to see you."

She glanced away. "I'm glad."

He got a kick out of her shyness. "You have no idea how much I want to kiss you right now."

She jerked her head up, her eyes wide. "You can't."

"I didn't say I would, only that I want to. How about I come by the cottage tonight? I'll bring pizza so you don't have to cook."

"What about your dad?"

He liked that she worried about everyone. "He's been invited to supper at Trent's house. So he's not being left out."

She nodded. "Then I think pizza sounds good. Heads up, Ryan only likes pepperoni."

"What do you like?" he asked.

She smiled. "More veggies than meat. But I can eat pretty much any toppings."

"How about six o'clock?"

"That's perfect."

Bill brought out his food just as the café door opened and customers filed in. "I need to get back to work." She stood and picked up her plate and cup. "I'll see you tonight."

He nodded and his gaze followed her as she walked back to the kitchen. Okay, he liked her. A lot. For the first time in a long time, he wanted to fit a woman into his life. The timing couldn't be worse. In about a month, he'd be out of a job.

After he finished eating, he got his second wind and walked back to the office. Inside, he found his deputies gathered about the dispatcher's desk along with a stranger. The man in his late fifties stood about five foot ten, with a stocky build and thinning gray hair. Sheriff Ted Carson.

The man put on a smile. "Hello, you must be Cullen Brannigan."

Cullen shook his hand. "Yes, nice to finally meet you,

Sheriff." He glanced around at his fellow officers. "As you can see, everyone's been missing you."

"That's nice to know. I'm surprised, because I've been told I'm a tyrant of a boss."

"Well, you ran a tight ship here." He eyed Brad, and his second in command began to issue everyone their duties for the shift.

Cullen turned back to the visitor. "Would you like to come back to your office, Sheriff?"

Ted Carson seemed indecisive about what to do.

"If you have some time, I have a couple of things I wanted to talk to you about."

The older man finally relented and together they went down the hall, but once inside the office, Ted refused the offer to sit behind the desk.

Cullen didn't have any problem. "So when are you expecting to come back?"

"I don't have a release from the doctor, so I'm not sure." His face brightened. "I hear you're doing an excellent job."

He had to admit he liked the praise. "You have a good staff here. And out of respect for you, they treat me the same way."

Ted shook his head. "Not true. If they didn't respect you, you'd have a mutiny on your hands. It's not easy to step in and be boss. Just the resentment alone can get to you. I'm glad everyone here is doing their jobs."

Cullen wasn't exactly sure where this conversation was going, but hoped the sheriff would let him know soon.

"Is there anything you need to ask me about the job?" Ted said.

Cullen tried not to react but gave him a smile. "About

a million questions, but I'll need to make a list. So can I get back to you?" he joked.

Ted nodded, then asked, "Are you thinking about going back to the Denver Police Department once your time is done here?"

Of course, Ted knew about his background. "No. I'm done with the big city and all the politics."

Ted laughed. "You know there's small-town politics, too. Son, you can't get away from it."

"I agree, but I'm tired of the fast pace. I want to slow down and enjoy life."

"I heard you inherited a nice piece of land here. The Robertsons' place."

"Yeah, but I don't think I want to raise cattle."

"Then lease the land, and find what you want to do."

He leaned back and realized that nearly everything he thought about lately had the possibility to include Shelby and Ryan. Trent was here, too. "You don't have to sell me on your town. I could see staying here. Maybe you could use an extra deputy when you return."

Ted arched an eyebrow. "With your experience, I think you should shoot higher than that."

AT ABOUT SIX O'CLOCK, Shelby was in the kitchen when she heard a knock on the front door.

"It's Cullen with pizza," Ryan called.

Heart racing, Shelby checked her appearance. She was wearing a pair of clean jeans and a blouse. She'd kept her hair in a ponytail, but had washed it when she'd showered after coming home earlier. Okay, she liked looking nice for the man.

She blew out a breath and walked into the living room. A sudden jolt hit her middle when Cullen looked at her.

He had shaven and his dark hair was combed back from his face. In his hand he balanced a huge pizza box.

"Hello, Shelby."

"Hi, Cullen. Did you get any sleep today?"

He shrugged. "Enough."

"Well, then we won't keep you too late."

"I'm off tomorrow, so I can sleep in."

"Then who's gonna feed the horses?" Ryan asked.

Cullen smiled. "Pops. He likes to get up early."

"I can help, too." Ryan turned toward her. "Can I help, too, Aunt Shellie?"

"You need to go to school. Now, why don't you go and wash up and we'll eat?"

The boy took off down the hall, leaving her alone with Cullen. He didn't hesitate as he came to her, lowered his head and kissed her, slow and easy, but making her ache for more. He pulled back. "I can't tell you how long I wanted to do that."

"Maybe we shouldn't. I'm not sure how Ryan will handle it."

Cullen frowned. "You mean he doesn't want me to like you?"

"No, but he's only five. He won't understand if we have to leave here."

His gaze roamed over her face. "Then don't leave. Stay. Bess and Bill want you to. I want you to."

Oh, dear Lord, so did she. "I don't want to go, either, but if Gil…" She'd kept her voice low so little ears couldn't hear.

"Stop letting that man decide your future."

Before she could respond, Ryan came running in. "I'm hungry."

"So am I," Cullen said and carried the box into the

kitchen. He placed it on the counter and opened the lid, and the most wonderful aroma wafted through the air.

Shelby groaned. "That smells heavenly." She looked down at the pie to see half was pepperoni only, and the other side was veggie. "Oh, Cullen. You didn't have to do this. What do you like?"

He leaned forward and whispered in her ear, "I'm not picky. I can eat either."

His warm breath against her ear caused warm shivers down her spine. "Thank you." She busied herself with getting a piece for Ryan, then watched as Cullen loaded up several pieces of both.

He grinned at her. "I skipped lunch."

She took a slice of veggie and they walked into the living room. As a special treat, Ryan got to eat in front of the television and watch a video, *Lion King*.

She looked at Cullen. "What would you like to drink? I bought some beer."

He smiled. "Sounds great."

She brought back two longnecks, then sat down on the sofa alongside him. She handed him one.

"Thank you."

"You're welcome."

They ate through most of the pizza. Shelby made a pig of herself, and could hardly move. With Cullen so close she didn't want to, either.

Once Ryan was finished with his meal, and engrossed in the movie, they could carry on a conversation. For tonight, they seemed like any typical family.

She had to stop that dream fast. She didn't need a man who was trying to find himself. Yet, Cullen Brannigan was exactly the man she wanted.

Cullen interrupted her thoughts. "Have you heard from Jeanie?"

"Oh, I forgot to tell you, Jeanie said that Luke can ride. She checked with the doctor to make sure that he would have enough support to hold him upright."

"Good. I'll make sure that we have enough spotters. How about we set up a time this weekend?"

"I have a catering job on Saturday, but I can do Sunday," she said.

"Good, I'll make sure I'm off, too. I'll get Trent, Kase and Dad to help, too."

"Would you mind if we have everyone stay for hot dogs and hamburgers afterward? Everyone has been so nice, and I want to return the favor. And I make a pretty good mac and cheese."

He smiled. "Sounds like a good idea. I need to return a few invitations, too. If you let Jeanie know our plans, I'll talk with Trent."

Cullen leaned back on the sofa and took a drink of beer. They were silent for a while, then he said, "Sheriff Carson came into the office today."

Shelby turned to him. "Really? Is he returning to work?" She felt panic creep into her stomach. Would Cullen be leaving?

He shook his head. "That's the funny part. I felt it was more than just to see his sister, and the deputies."

"How long were you contracted to be interim sheriff?"

"Three months. I'm about two months in."

She could stay and he would leave. She didn't like the reality.

Cullen went on to say, "He also asked me if I was going back to Denver. I told him, no, and I jokingly asked if he had any deputy positions open."

She got a little excited. "You're staying in Hidden Springs?"

He shrugged. "I've been thinking about it…lately. I

mean I have the ranch here, and some horses." His gaze met hers. "And you and Ryan are here." He winked. "And I'm your landlord."

She was thrilled. "I'm glad you want to stay."

When he pulled her into his arms and kissed her, she knew that he was telling her the truth. She pushed aside any doubt about starting a relationship. Being in Cullen's arms made her realize it was worth taking the chance.

Chapter Fifteen

Sunday was bright and sunny, the temperature above normal for the early spring. Perfect for horseback riding. As Shelby led Cloud around the arena with Ryan, Addy was on Danny Boy and led by her dad, Kase, and Noah was on Dakota with Neal.

Yet, most of the attention was focused on Trent and Cullen as they led the gentle black mare Sassy Girl, who was carrying Luke. The ten-year-old was strapped securely in the high-back therapy saddle that helped support the boy's frail spine. With a big grin on his face, Luke rode around the corral, and managed a weak wave at his encouraging parents. Jeanie and John were standing on the ramp snapping pictures with their phones.

Shelby found she was tearing up over the scene, especially when Cullen led Sassy over next to his brother and they rode side by side. Cullen also had more activities planned for the afternoon. There were tall wooden stands in the arena and attached were small flags. She had no idea where these came from.

Most likely Cullen built them. Then he explained to each child what to do.

The idea was when the horses rode by, they were to grab a Velcro flag. There were more smiles and cheers as each horse rode by the pole. Then came Luke's turn.

As Sassy approached the pole, Neal tilted it until the flag was right in front of the boy's hand. Despite Luke's limited mobility, he managed to reach for the red banner and grasp it. He held it up as his brother, Noah, cheered along with the other kids.

Cullen stood in the middle of the arena. "Who wants to go faster?"

All the kids raised their hands and cheered again.

"Okay, let's race."

All the horses were lined up, and the pole at the other end now had plastic rings on hooks. "Okay, we're going to ride to the pole, grab a ring and come back." Cullen walked past each helmeted child, showing them how to grip their hand on the saddle horn. She couldn't help but notice how reassuring he was with each child. Darn the man if he hadn't made her care about him even more.

Cullen strolled past her and winked. "Be careful and don't drop it," he instructed the kids. "Keep your eyes on the ring."

Neal was the first to go with Noah. He took off and Pops ran with the horse, with two spotters on either side of the boy. Everyone yelled encouragement when Noah rode down and grabbed his ring, then came back. Everyone got a chance to go and get a ring. Luke was even walked down.

"You can do it, Luke," Noah called to his brother. "Get a red one."

Sassy Girl was walked really close to the pole, and with help from Cullen Luke got a ring, too.

With exhausted kids and handlers, the afternoon riding session came to a successful end. The horses were taken back to the barn, fed and put away for the night. Then everyone went up to the main house.

Addy took charge of the kids and put on a video for

everyone to watch. Even Luke seemed to be entertained for a while, then he went to sleep in his chair.

Cullen came up to her in the kitchen. "Thank you for doing this today."

She looked at the handsome cowboy and suddenly wished they were alone. "You're doing all the work, and this is your house. I'm only adding a few salads."

"What I mean is, I'm glad you're here with me."

His remark threw her, then he lowered his head and placed a soft kiss on her lips. He pulled back, picked up the tray of hamburgers and hot dogs and walked out the back door.

Shelby stood there at the sink thrilled but confused about what to do about the man.

"Feeling a little dazed, are you?"

She turned to find Jeanie smiling at her.

There was no reason to lie. "Yeah, you could say that."

Jeanie came up to her. "I think the sheriff is smitten with you."

Shelby wasn't sure what to say. "It would be complicated to get involved."

"Sweetie, don't look now, but it's already happened." Jeanie leaned against the counter. "Word around town is that Sheriff Brannigan is a good guy. He proved that with what he did today for the kids, especially my boys."

Shelby nodded, seeing Jeanie blink at her tears. "I know." She remembered what Cullen had told her about volunteering with kids in Denver.

"You know what they say, you trust a man who is liked by kids and animals."

Before Shelby could remark on the comment, she heard more voices. She looked up to see Laurel pushing a stroller into the kitchen.

Shelby smiled. "Oh, Laurel, you brought the babies."

She rushed over to the new mother and hugged her. Jeanie did the same since they knew each other from church.

Shelby couldn't resist and peered into the stroller at the two sleeping babies, one in pink and the other in blue.

"Oh, they are so precious."

Addy suddenly appeared next to her, and whispered, "That's because they're sleeping. But they cry a lot until Mommy feeds them."

Shelby glanced at Laurel sitting in the chair.

She was a beautiful woman with her blond hair and green eyes. Even after the recent birth, she was slender.

"I'm hoping for a few hours before that happens," Laurel said. "Besides going to the doctor, this is my first official outing. I'm exhausted just getting us all ready." She turned her attention to her stepdaughter, Addy, and smiled. "I heard from your dad that you did really good today and were helpful with the other kids."

The cute blonde nodded. "I showed Noah and Ryan how to hold the reins. Sheriff Cullen played games with us, and Luke got to play, too."

"That's wonderful." Laurel looked at Jeanie. "So the saddle worked."

Jeanie nodded. "It seemed to. It's a little big, but Cullen and Trent made some adjustments." She reached in her pocket and pulled out her phone. "I got pictures."

Laurel's green eyes widened, and she went to her. "Oh, let me see."

The twosome went over the photos when Jeanie said, "I hope Cullen doesn't mind, but I'm going to put one in the local paper. He was wonderful to do this today. I've never seen Luke so animated." Her voice got hoarse with emotion. "My boys got to do something together. You don't know how important it was that they got to share this day. It was awesome!"

Laurel hugged her. "Then we're going to have to make sure they do it again." She looked at Shelby. "You know, Dad can volunteer sometime, too. He's already talking with Neal about next time."

Shelby hoped that Cullen was as enthusiastic about a next time, too. All she knew was she liked the house filled with people. Not just any people, but friends and family. She could get used to this, if she let herself. Did she dare?

LATER THAT NIGHT, Cullen stood on the porch with Shelby watching as the last truck pulled out and headed for home. He had to admit he was tired, but in a good way.

He wrapped his arm around Shelby's shoulders and pulled her close. "Are you tired?"

"A little, but everyone helped with the food, so the kitchen is all cleaned up. Everything is done."

She started to pull away, but he stopped her. "Not exactly." He drew her closer, then dipped his head toward hers. "There's this."

His mouth covered hers in a slow, easy kiss that sure had his gut tightening. With Shelby in his arms it didn't take much. Her arms went around his neck, and she pressed her sweet body against his, driving his need.

He broke off the kiss. "Damn, woman. I can't take much more." He grabbed her hand and pulled her inside. "C'mon, I need to get you home before I carry you off and have my way with you."

Hand in hand they walked through the front door and into the family room, where his dad sat watching television. "Where's Ryan?" she asked.

"He's upstairs in his old room. He said he wanted to sleep in his old bed because Addy was going to sleep over at her grandparents' house." The older Brannigan looked at Shelby. "I said I'd ask you if it was okay."

"Oh, Neal. You've already been so generous to watch Ryan, you don't need to do this."

"You act like it's a hardship. It's not. Ryan is a great little boy. I think he only wants what other kids have." He smiled. "I have no problem filling in as a grandpa." He glanced at his son. "I hope you can remember the days when I was a pretty good dad to you and Austin."

Cullen didn't know what to say to that. But Shelby quickly stepped in. "I'll go up and check on him."

After she left the room, Cullen turned back to his father. "Of course I remember those days, but I also remember the bad ones, too." He wanted to believe the man, but so many times he'd let him down.

"I understand, son. I have a lot to make up for, and I'm gonna do my darnedest." He blinked. "Losing Leslie made me realize how I've turned my back on everyone. I've made a lot of mistakes over the years, and I especially turned away from you and your brother. I'm sorry, son."

Shelby came down the steps. "He's sound asleep. I'll come by early before work."

"Why don't I just take him to school in the morning?" Cullen suggested. "Then he won't have to get up so early. Give me a change of clothes, and he has a toothbrush upstairs already."

Before Shelby could argue, Cullen tugged on her arm and they started out of the room. "I'm walking Shelby home," he called to his father. "And I'll get Ryan's clothes for tomorrow."

"Take your time." Neal waved. "Thank you for today, Shelby, and all the delicious food."

She stopped in the doorway. "Thank you for your help

and for keeping Ryan. He enjoys spending time with you."

Cullen caught a flash of emotion play across his father's face. "You're welcome."

"Good night, Dad," he said, then he walked Shelby out the back door. If it were up to him, he wouldn't come back to the house until morning.

At the cottage door, Shelby took out her key and unlocked the door. She started to turn on the light, but Cullen's hand stopped her. "Do we really need lights?" he whispered against her ear.

Unable to speak, she shook her head. She felt his arms turn her around, and his head dipped down. He dotted kisses across her face until he found her mouth. This was a bad idea, but somehow she wasn't listening to common sense and allowed him to back her inside and shut the door.

"Did I tell you how much I enjoyed today, especially the part about being with you?"

She nodded.

He kissed her again. "I want to make love to you, Shelby. If you don't want the same things, then tell me now, and I'll walk out this door."

She couldn't find enough air to breathe let alone speak. Instead, she ran her hands over his chest, then around his neck before she kissed him. It was quick and hard, and full of meaning.

She fought to keep from telling him her true feelings, but she knew there couldn't be any promises between them. One night had to be enough, for now. "I want you to stay…and make love to me."

He swung her into his arms and carried her down the hall in the darkness. He walked into her room and set her down next to the bed. Then he kissed her, long and hard, relaying his need for her. He cupped her face. "I never wanted a woman as much as I want you right now."

She shivered at his words. "I want you, too."

Her hands worked their way to his shirt and began to tug the tails from his jeans, then popped the snaps, revealing his chest. Her fingers found their way through the dark hair, and she felt him tense as her nails moved along his skin.

"You're not playing fair."

He returned the favor and began removing her blouse. Soon, his hands moved upward over her stomach to her breasts, then unhooked the clasp on her bra. Her breathing grew rapid as his fingers toyed with her sensitive nipples. She moaned in pleasure and gripped his forearms to help keep herself upright.

"Cullen…"

"I'm right here, Shelby," he breathed against her mouth. "I need you."

He stepped back and helped her remove the rest of her clothes, then placed her on the bed. He stepped back and quickly kicked off his boots, then stripped off his jeans and underwear, and joined her on the mattress.

He lay beside her and drew her close, so she could feel the heat of his body. "You take my breath away."

She reached for him. "I need you, Cullen," she breathed against his tempting mouth. The realization of how she felt about this man was hard to keep secret. She was falling in love. She closed her eyes and let all her troubles slip out of her mind and let Cullen take her to paradise.

Two hours later, Cullen lay on his side and watched as Shelby slept. He ached to touch her, to arouse her, to give her pleasure, then make love to her again.

Just the memories of their joining had his body stirred

up again. Yet, he couldn't start anything, knowing she had to get up for work in a few hours. She needed her sleep. When had he become such a martyr?

Not to disturb her, he carefully climbed out of bed. Then he slipped on his jeans and shirt, then carried his boots out of the room. He shut the door and walked across the hall to Ryan's bedroom. After he finished dressing, he turned on the light, then opened the drawer and took out some clean jeans, a shirt and some underwear and socks for the boy. He started to leave when he spotted the familiar picture book on the dresser.

Curiosity got the best of him and he opened the book, wanting to see pictures of Shelby and her family. He got to the first page, a little ragged from the child's fingers. He studied the photo of a baby, which was probably Ryan. The next photo was that of a handsome man in a military uniform, Sergeant First Class Josh Hughes. Sadness rushed through Cullen as he examined the picture that resembled Ryan so much. And a little boy who would never get to know his father.

He sat down on the bed and flipped to the next picture of a pretty blonde with big eyes who had to be Georgia Hughes. The next picture was of mother and son.

He heard his name, then the door opened and he saw Shelby standing there in a sleep shirt. His body came to full alert.

"I was getting some clothes for Ryan."

"Why didn't you wake me?" She came in and sat down next to him.

"Because I can handle packing up his clothes. And you need sleep." He held up the photo album. "I thought Ryan might need this book, too."

"Yes, but I don't let him take it to school. Sometimes he gets upset when he looks at the pictures. I know he misses his mother, but sometimes the memories make it worse."

She began to flip through the book, and he saw her sadness as she looked at her sister's photo. "It was such a tragedy. Georgia was so young. She was a good person, and mother, a schoolteacher. Gil shouldn't have done what he did." She brushed away a tear. "He killed her, I know it. I just wish we could find what he wants so badly."

He pulled her close, kissed her forehead and inhaled her intoxicating scent. She smelled of him and her all mixed together, reminding him that they'd made love not long ago. He wanted her again, but that couldn't happen tonight.

He stood and pulled her up, too. "Now I need to go, and you should go back to bed and get some sleep."

She tugged on his arm. "Why don't you stay and we'll sleep here together?"

He groaned, wanting her more than his next breath. "You know we won't sleep."

She reached up, and her hands linked around his neck. "That's what I'm counting on, Sheriff."

Chapter Sixteen

Just before dawn, Cullen walked Shelby out to her car. After sharing a heated kiss, he'd reluctantly released her so she could go to work. With a wave, he watched her car pull out of the drive. He walked into the house, where he found his father in the kitchen. Even though he was thirty-two years old, he suddenly felt like a teenager getting caught coming in after curfew.

"Morning, son."

He put Ryan's change of clothes on the table. "Morning, Dad."

His father handed him a mug filled with coffee and paused to study him. "I'm glad you found Shelby. If my opinion matters, I think she's pretty special."

Cullen wasn't sure he wanted this conversation. "Yes, she is special." He took a sip of coffee. "She's been dealt some tough breaks in her life. I'm not sure if I'm the man she needs."

"Why would you say that? You're a good man." His father frowned. "You were handed a raw deal in Denver—and yes, I'll regret until my dying day that I didn't back you up. I put the department first." His watery gaze met Cullen's. "You're my son. I'm sorry I wasn't there for you."

Cullen never realized how much those words meant to him until now. "Thanks, Dad."

His dad sniffed. "Okay, one more piece of advice and I'll keep my mouth shut. Don't make the same mistake I did. Let Shelby know how you feel about her." He put down his mug. "Now I better go feed the horses."

Before Cullen could respond, his father was out the door, but his words hung in the air. He couldn't deny that he cared about Shelby and Ryan, but he still had the same problem. He wasn't sure what was going to happen with his future.

He headed up the steps to the second floor. His thoughts turned to the woman he'd held in his arms all night. It wasn't just the incredible sex, but all the time he'd spent with her and Ryan. He was getting used to having Shelby with him. Even his family loved her, and already claimed her as part of the clan. So why was he holding back? Maybe he needed to convince her to take a chance on an ex-cop with no job.

After he'd showered and dressed for work, he woke up Ryan. The boy seemed happy, and not at all worried about not being home with his aunt. Cullen helped him shower and get dressed for school, then came downstairs for some breakfast.

Cullen walked to the stove. "I can't cook like Aunt Shellie, but I can scramble eggs and make toast."

Ryan smiled. "I like eggs."

A few minutes later, Cullen scooped the scrambled eggs onto a plate and took them to Ryan.

The boy picked up his fork and began to eat. "Are you taking me to school?"

Cullen nodded and sat down at the table next to the boy. "If you want we can stop by the café to see your aunt."

The boy smiled. "Yes, I want to see her."

"Then we'll go there." Cullen noticed the boy's photo

album on the table. "I brought your picture book from your room."

Ryan picked up the album and quickly began flipping through the pages as if he needed reassurance they were all there.

Cullen was careful how to broach the subject of his parents. "I saw your dad's picture," Cullen said. "He was a really brave soldier."

Ryan turned to Josh Hughes's picture. The child's feet swung back and forth under his chair. "Mommy said he's a hero. I have his flag, too."

Sadness washed over him. How awful that a child had the flag that had draped his father's casket. "I'm sorry your dad and mom aren't here with you."

Ryan looked up, his eyes wide with wonder. "They're in heaven. They watch me every day." He shook his head. "And no more mean people can hurt them ever."

Cullen frowned. Could the child have information about Gil? "Do you know who these mean people are?"

Ryan opened the book again and began to turn the pages, then stopped at a picture of Ryan and his mother. Cullen examined the photo closely and saw two men in the background. One definitely was Gil Bryant.

"He was mean to Mommy," Ryan said. "He hit her and she cried."

Cullen tensed. He wanted to get his hands on the man. "I'm sorry."

He looked back at the picture to examine the other man, a shorter, thin guy with long, stringy blond hair. What stood out was the large tattoo on his forearm. It looked like a snake.

"Do you know this man?"

"He's a bad man." He pointed to Gil as tears welled in his eyes. "He hurt Mommy's face. I got scared."

Enough. Cullen closed the album. He reached out and hugged the child close against his chest, feeling the tightening around his heart. If only he could take away his pain.

"It's okay, Ryan. The bad guy isn't going to hurt you. I won't let him."

The boy pulled back and wiped his eyes. "That's 'cause you're the sheriff."

Cullen wished he had the special powers the boy thought he had. He made the promise to the boy, but also to Shelby. It was the only way they could have a future together.

ABOUT SEVEN THIRTY, Shelby should be busy filling her breakfast orders, but she managed to find time to daydream. After spending the most incredible night with Cullen, how could she not? Now the problem was she had to work harder at not making too much of it.

She recalled her grandmother's words from long ago. *"If you make it too easy for a man, they won't work for it."*

She smiled at the precious memory of the times spent in her grandma's kitchen. She missed those days when she had someone to talk to. The years in foster care she was so lonely, wishing her sister had been with her. Sometimes her insides had ached so badly she wanted to cry. Then years later, she found Georgia, only to lose her again. She'd been blessed with Ryan. And now, a wonderful man had come into her life, and the feelings he'd caused scared her. Last night, she gave him more than her body.

She gave him her heart.

Worse she didn't even know how Cullen felt. Okay, she knew the man cared about her. But for how long? He was here in town temporarily. Would he pick up and move for another job? She couldn't do that anymore. She needed roots, for herself and especially for Ryan.

She dipped slices of bread into the French toast batter, then placed them on the griddle. After she scooped scrambled eggs onto a plate, added bacon and wheat toast, she set the plate on the counter window. With a tap of the bell, she called out, "Order up."

She pulled new orders from the rounder and began to fill them when the back screen door opened and Ryan rushed in followed by Cullen.

She took a moment to enjoy him in his sheriff's uniform. Then she quickly recalled that incredible body not hidden by clothes. She felt heat rise to her face as she caught his gaze.

Darn the man knew what she was thinking.

"Hi, Aunt Shellie." Ryan ran to her. "I missed you."

She hugged him. "Bless your heart, I missed you, too." She kissed his cheek. "Did you like sleeping over at Cullen's house?"

He nodded. "Pops took care of me good. And Cullen made me breakfast."

She glanced at the sheriff, and felt a tightening in her stomach. Darn the sexy man. "Maybe I should have him cook for me."

He gave her a sexy grin. "Anytime, darlin', anytime." He leaned toward her and placed a kiss on her lips.

She sucked in a breath and glanced around. Then she realized it didn't really make any difference who saw them together. "Good morning."

He kept his voice low. "It would have been much better if I didn't have to leave you this morning."

Her eyes widened, and she felt the heat rise to her cheeks. "I... I need to check my food." She walked over to the grill and flipped her toast, and checked her hash brown potatoes. Then she glanced at her orders and began to fill the plates. After she put them on the counter and rang the bell, she turned to Cullen and Ryan.

"You sure you don't mind taking Ryan to school?"

"Of course I don't."

Ryan tugged on her cook's smock. "Sheriff Cullen is coming to my class and the kids get to sit in his patrol car."

"Wow, that sounds like fun."

The order bell rang again, announcing she had more breakfast orders. "Sorry, I need to get back to work." She leaned down and kissed Ryan, then snuck one in for Cullen, too. "See you later."

Cullen leaned in. "I'm planning on it." He winked, then left.

She realized the tightness in her chest was seeing how wonderful Cullen was to Ryan. She didn't want to think about anything else except the happiness she felt for those two guys who just walked out. Did she dare think about a possible future together?

CULLEN GOT TO the station by eight o'clock.

Brad Rogers greeted him first. "Morning, Sheriff. I didn't know you were scheduled today."

"Morning, Brad. I thought I'd come in and handle some paperwork. How did things go on the last shift?" He figured it was a good night since he hadn't been called out. "Any problems?"

"Two minor accidents on the highway. An attempted break-in at Hometown Hardware Store on Main Street. Turned out to be some broken window glass that set off the alarm. It was probably done by kids." He handed him the copy of the report.

"Thanks."

"Do you want to handle the day shift briefing?"

Cullen shook his head. "No, you can do it." He hung around as Brad did a short briefing with the day shift them sent them off on patrol.

When Cullen started back to his office, Brad called to him. "I heard Noah and Luke Phelps went riding yesterday at your ranch."

Word sure travels fast. He nodded. "I have a collection of rescued equines living in my barn that can use some exercise. Great horses for kids. And since Laurel Rawlins found a therapy saddle, we had the opportunity…"

Brad smiled. "If you decide to have another riding day again, I could help out." He rushed on to add, "That is, if you need anyone."

Cullen worked to hide his surprise. "Thanks, Brad, maybe I will. We're talking about in a week or so. I'll let you know." He turned and walked inside his office. Maybe the men were beginning to accept him.

After closing the door for privacy, he took the photo album out of his jacket pocket and tossed it on the desk. He sat down and got out the number for the Dawkins Meadow Police Department. When the dispatcher answered, he asked for Captain Kershaw.

"Kershaw."

"Hello, Captain, this is Sheriff Brannigan in Hidden Springs."

"Hello, Sheriff. I still don't have anything else to report on the Hughes case."

Cullen flipped through the photo book. "I think I might have something here that might help in the investigation." He went on to explain about Ryan's pictures. "I have a photo of Georgia and her son. In the background there are some interesting-looking people. One is Gil Bryant, and he's talking with a younger man who looks to be about thirty years old. He has long white-blond hair down to his shoulders. The one thing that stands out is a large tattoo on his right forearm. It looks like a snake."

The captain cursed. "That's a description of Whitey Briggs. His full name is Robert William Briggs."

"Hold on," Cullen said as he went to his computer and typed in the name William Briggs. After a few seconds the familiar picture came up, and with a long arrest record. "That's him. He's the one in the photo with Bryant."

"That still doesn't prove anything against Bryant. Gil could explain it away by saying he was just questioning him."

The captain might not be able to prove anything, but Cullen had no doubt now that someone broke into the cottage last week. Still a mystery on what they'd been looking for.

"Briggs is in our system," the captain said. "Last week he was picked up on a drug possession charge. It could be serious considering the amount of contraband we found on him. Although he talks a big game, he's still a small fish in a big cesspool of dealers." There was a long pause. "I'd sure like to break the chain that leads to our town."

"Could you make a deal with him if he gave up Bryant?"

"I need to talk to the DA first. Send me a copy of that picture and I'll see what I can come up with."

After Cullen hung up the phone, he pulled the picture from the album to scan it so he could email it. He flipped it over and put it in the machine and saw the writing on the back. There were some numbers that didn't mean anything to him. Had Georgia threatened Bryant, saying she had some kind of proof? Had she proof of his corruption?

Maybe Cullen was grasping at nothing, but anything was better than waiting to see if the man would show up in Hidden Springs. He would do everything he could to protect Shelby and Ryan, but he couldn't be with them all the time.

Worse, what if fear drove Shelby from town? He might never see her again. No. He wouldn't let that happen.

THAT EVENING, CULLEN got home about five. He'd spent most of the afternoon looking over arrest records. He liked using his investigating skills again. He'd discovered that Dawkins Meadow was not your picture-perfect small town. Now, how much of this information should he tell Shelby? He didn't want to get her hopes up yet, or put her in any further danger. So for now, he needed to handle this and hope she would understand.

When he climbed out of the truck, he saw his dad with Ryan and Shelby out at the corral. His dad was leading Ryan around the arena.

With a quick wave to the threesome, he went into the house and changed into jeans and his boots, then hurried out to join them. He came across the compound to Shelby standing on the ramp. One look at her and he couldn't prevent the flood of memories from last night.

He pulled her into his arms and kissed her. He wanted to shut out the rest of the world and lose himself in this woman, but reality quickly invaded their world.

Shelby smiled. "That's quite a welcome, Sheriff."

"Yeah, you could say I missed you a little bit today."

"I missed you, too."

He had to glance away from her tempting mouth. "I'm glad Dad got Ryan out to ride." He nodded toward the arena, but kept his arms around her shoulder. "They work well together, don't they?"

"Yes, Pops has been great." She sighed. "You both

have been so helpful with Ryan. And I appreciate it so much."

He hugged her close. "It's been easy, especially since he has such a great-looking aunt who I happen to be crazy about." He grew serious. "I couldn't stop thinking about you today."

Her gaze met his shyly. "I guess I thought about you a few times, too."

He kissed her on her nose, realizing he'd hated being separated from her. "I've got a lot of ideas of what we could do together."

She sobered and pulled away. "I have no doubt you do, Cullen. But for now, we'll need to slow down. We don't know what the future holds." She didn't need to say anything about the man who'd threatened her. Gil Bryant prevented them from having a future.

"It's going to be okay, Shelby. Trust me."

Ryan called to him. "Cullen, you need to watch me."

Cullen turned toward the corral as his father led Cloud toward the ramp. "Okay, we're watching."

With the horse next to the newly built ramp, Ryan swung his leg over the saddle and climbed off the horse. A big grin lit up the five-year-old's face. "See, I did it."

"You sure did. High five." He held up a hand, and the boy smacked it.

"And I can get back on, too."

"Wow! You've been working hard."

The child nodded. "Pops helped me."

After a few missed attempts, and much encouragement, the boy managed to mount the small horse and showed off another toothy smile.

Cullen had lost his heart not only to Shelby, but to Ryan, too. He wanted to continue to be there for them both, be a part of their lives. And the only way was to close the door to the threats against them.

Once the boy rode back into the corral area, he leaned against the railing next to Shelby. "I need to go out of town for a day or two."

She looked at him. "Are you going back to Denver?"

He couldn't lie. "No, but I need to check out some other options." Damn, he hated this, but if he told her she'd want to come along. "Trust me, I'm coming back. This is something I need to do for me, and for us."

Those big blue eyes locked on his. "For us?"

He nodded. "Yes, this is for us, Shelby. And when I get back we need to talk."

She shook her head. "You don't have to…"

He leaned down, and his mouth caressed hers. "I want you to know that you and Ryan mean a lot to me. So don't go thinking I don't care because I do. And soon I'm going to tell you how much."

"I care about you, too. So don't be gone too long." She hugged him close. "You gonna miss me?"

"Oh, sweetheart, you have no idea."

Chapter Seventeen

Just before sunrise the following morning, Cullen came downstairs carrying his duffel bag. He needed to see his dad before he caught his flight out of Grand Junction. Although his father knew he was going out of town, he didn't know the entire story.

He hated being secretive about this trip, but he gave his word to Kershaw not to discuss the case. The man was going to meet his plane, and they were going to figure out this puzzle.

He walked into the kitchen with his bag and found his father at the counter. "Morning, Dad."

"Hi, son. You ready to go?"

"Pretty soon." Cullen went to the coffeemaker and poured a cup. "Dad, can I ask you a favor?"

His father leaned back against the tiled counter. Dressed in jeans and a chambray shirt, he looked the furthest thing from a cop as possible.

"Sure, what do you need?"

"Keep an eye on Shelby and Ryan while I'm gone. I mean a close watch."

Neal frowned. "Then why are you leaving? And don't tell me some rubbish about a job offer."

"Okay, I've learned some information about Gil." He raised a hand to stop any protest. "It's all speculation right now, but I need to go to Kentucky. And I don't want Shelby involved any more than she already is."

"Did you tell her about this new info?"

Cullen shook his head. "I plan to tell her everything once I get back."

Neal sighed. "I know you don't want my opinion, but I'm going to give it anyway. If you care about Shelby, be truthful. Believe me, women don't like to be left in the dark."

"I'm doing this to protect them," he stressed. "Because I care about her and Ryan a lot."

Neal Brannigan held up his hands in surrender. "Okay, I can see I'm not going to change your mind, so I'll just say be careful. I know you're an experienced cop, but this guy has already killed once, that we know of."

"I will." Choked with emotions, he could barely get the words out, but they needed to be said. "I'm glad you're here, Dad, and not just to help out. It's been nice to be able to spend time with you."

His father nodded. "I'm glad I'm here, too, son." He paused, then said, "I know I can't make up the past to you and your brother, but I'm hoping you give me another chance."

"I'd like that." And he meant it. He wanted to rebuild their relationship.

"I should head out to the barn." His dad started toward the back door, but made a detour and pulled his son into a tight embrace. "Have a safe trip." He held on a second longer, then said in a husky tone, "I love you, son."

The wall between them for years suddenly came tumbling down. "Love you, too, Dad."

After finishing his coffee, Cullen grabbed his bag and walked out to his truck. After tossing it into the backseat, he stared at the lights on in the cottage. He knew Shelby was up, getting ready for work.

Damn, he needed to tell her.

He slammed the truck door, walked up to the door and knocked softly. "Shelby, it's me, Cullen."

Shelby opened the door with a smile. She was already dressed in black pants and a cook's smock for work. He leaned in and kissed her.

"Not that I don't like seeing you again, but I thought you'd be on the way to the airport."

"I needed to talk to you first." He walked inside, then blurted out, "I'm flying to Louisville to meet with Captain Kershaw."

She frowned. "Isn't he in charge of Georgia's case?"

He nodded. "I found some information that might help the case."

Her smiled faded. "What kind of information?"

He went on to explain about the picture in Ryan's album and the numbers on the back. "I don't know what they mean. That's the reason I need to go to Dawkins Meadow."

"But if Gil knows you're snooping around, he's not going to like it. Cullen, those men he associates with mean business."

"Shelby, I have to do something. He's a threat to you and Ryan. You can't move forward because every day you wonder if you're going to have to take off."

She didn't say anything, and he went to her. "I'm not going to let the man hurt either one of you. I care too much. That's why I have to go and check this out."

"Let Captain Kershaw handle it," she said, her voice loud and agitated. "I don't want you hurt in the mess."

Suddenly Ryan raced into the room, crying out, "No,

Cullen, don't go. The mean man will hurt you. I don't want you to die, too."

Cullen knelt down and caught the boy in an embrace. "Ryan, I'm not going to get hurt. But it's my job to find the bad man and arrest him. He needs to go to jail so he won't hurt any more people."

The child wiped his tears off his cheeks. "'Cause you're the sheriff?"

Cullen exchanged a glance with Shelby. "Yes, because I'm the sheriff, and I need to protect people from bad men. I need your help, too." He suddenly had an idea and took the photo out of his pocket. "I borrowed your picture because I need to find something." He turned it over to the back. "Did you see your mother write down these numbers?"

He hesitated, then nodded. "She had to hide something important." His blue eyes were wide. "She said it was a special hiding place and to never, ever tell anybody."

Shelby sat down on the sofa, and had Ryan sit next to her. "I know you promised your mom, but if we want to help Sheriff Cullen to get the bad man, you need to tell us. Was there something hidden in your old house?"

Ryan nodded. "In my bedroom. Where my clothes are."

Cullen crouched down in front of the boy. "In the closet?"

He nodded. "There's a hole in the floor and she put a sack inside. She said that the bad man wouldn't bother us because we had the secret."

Cullen hugged the child to him. "I'm sorry, Ryan. Your mother was so brave, and so are you. I'm so proud of you."

"Are you going to get the bad guy so Aunt Shellie and I can live here forever?"

Cullen liked the sound of that. Yet seeing Shelby's face, he knew he still had a lot of convincing to do. "I'll do my best to make that happen."

HOURS LATER, AFTER Captain Bill Kershaw had picked Cullen up at the Louisville airport, the two drove to a coffee shop just out of Dawkins Meadow. They needed to keep the meeting low-key, not wanting anyone to speculate about the stranger who came to visit.

Kershaw gave a quick overview of what had been going on in his town, from two cops taking bribes to the increase in drug sales. He'd been investigating Bryant on his own.

"As you know being a cop undercover, the bad guys come in and before you know it, you're caught up in it, and there's no way out." He raised a hand. "I'm not making any excuses, especially for an animal like Bryant. He's the worst of the worst, not only because he entrapped some of his fellow officers to get them to work for him, but because he's abused women. And not just Georgia Hughes."

Kershaw took a drink of coffee. "After your call last night with the boy's information, I contacted a friend I know from the DEA. At this point, Sheriff, we don't know the good guys from the bad guys."

Cullen was glad they weren't handling this alone. He was just a civilian in this state, not even able to carry a gun. All he was doing was making sure whatever was hidden in the house was enough to put away Gil Bryant. Then Shelby and Ryan could move on with their lives. He prayed he could be a part of that.

"When do we get to go to the house?"

"I'm hoping soon." Kershaw checked his watch, and his phone rang, and he answered it, saying only a few words. "We need to head over there. I got a search warrant, along with permission and keys from the landlord. The DEA agents are already in place just in case."

"What about Bryant?" Cullen didn't want him showing up unexpectedly, or worse, to disappear. Then Shelby would never be free of his threats. "Is he on duty today?"

"Yes, but I have him transporting a prisoner. So right now, he's headed out of town. If we find anything today, we'll bring him in."

Kershaw stood. "Are you ready?"

"Oh, yeah. I'll follow your lead."

His thoughts turned to Shelby. He sent up another prayer, hoping they could end this nightmare today.

It took only thirty minutes to get to the house. With the instructions Ryan had given Cullen, they went into the child's bedroom, empty now, except for a twin bed.

Wearing gloves, the DEA agent took over and opened the closet door. As with the instructions on the back of the picture, they counted the number of hardwood boards and found a raised nail. Once the board was pried back, they found a plastic bag.

Inside was a notebook with names and locations where drugs were to be dropped. The agent spoke about the findings. "Seems Bryant had kept his own insurance. Wow, this is like a gift from the grave."

They also found a note in Georgia Hughes's handwriting, saying that she'd been stalked and abused by Gil Bryant. She had photos displaying her bruised face; each one was dated. She also stated that she was leaving town to start a new life, and if she ended up dead, her killer was Gil Bryant. In addition, there was an envelope addressed to Shelby. Of course, that was evidence, too.

Cullen's emotions were filled with anger, then sadness, but mostly respect for this brave woman. Georgia Hughes might not have been able to fight back physically, but she wasn't going to let Bryant get away.

Kershaw came over to him as he got off the phone, his expression grave. "The Feds sent a car to go pick up

Bryant. Somehow, he must have heard about the investigation and was packing to leave town. When the officers got inside they found him dead with a single gunshot to the head. We're not sure if it was in retaliation or self-inflicted."

Cullen wished he could be sorry. All he could think about was Shelby. Her days of running were over.

SHELBY SAT ACROSS from Ryan at the kitchen table. He'd been quiet all day, didn't even talk about his day in school. She was worried because she knew he could go back into his shell. That was the last thing she wanted to happen. He'd come so far since their move here, and she didn't want him to close up again.

It was obvious what he was worried about. "Ryan, are you worried about Cullen?"

He gave a big nod. "I want him to come home."

She hoped for the same thing. "He will be, soon. He's helping another policeman to look for what your mother hid in the closet."

"Then he'll come home?"

She prayed she was telling the truth. "Yes. He'll be home."

That got a smile from her nephew. "I'm glad. I want him to take me riding again."

She'd forgotten all about the weekend planned with Luke and Noah.

"Aunt Shellie, do you miss him?"

She smiled. "Yes, I do."

"Are you going to marry Cullen? Then we can be a family."

Suddenly her nephew had become a chatterbox. "Oh, honey, I don't know."

"You kissed him. Mommy said grown-ups do that when they like each other."

Shelby worked to hide her smile. "Well, that's true, and I like Cullen well enough…" Suddenly her phone rang, saving her from having to answer. She glanced at the ID to see Cullen's name.

"It's Cullen." She answered the phone. "Hi…"

"Hi to you, too."

"How are you?"

"I'm fine now that I'm talking to you."

Excitement rushed through her. She wanted to turn away and have a private conversation, but Ryan needed some reassurance.

"I think there's someone here who would like to talk to you. He's been worried, too."

"Put me on speaker, and I'll talk to both of you."

She touched the button. "Here, Ryan, Cullen wants to talk to you."

"Hey, buddy," Cullen said. "How are you?"

"Fine. When are you coming home?"

"Soon. I'm trying for late tonight, or tomorrow."

The boy nodded. "Did you get the bad man?"

Shelby tensed, waiting for the answer.

"Yes, the police captured the bad man who…hurt your mom. What you told me about the secret closet helped us catch him. I'm so proud of you, Ryan. You did a brave thing."

The boy blinked back tears. "I'm glad, 'cause I don't want him to hurt any more mommies."

She heard the roughness in Cullen's voice. "He won't, son. I promise." There was a long pause, then he said, "Now I need to talk to your aunt Shellie."

"Okay, goodbye," the boy said, then he took off down the hall to his bedroom.

Shelby turned off the speaker and put the phone to her ear. "Thank you for talking to him. I think it's important to know he helped you. And he trusted you enough to share his story."

"Ryan did help, Shelby. Without him, we wouldn't have found the evidence for a case. They picked up Whitey Briggs, too, and he couldn't talk fast enough." Cullen went on to explain what happened about finding the notebook. "The DA is going through all the evidence now. It's over, Shelby."

She sank into the chair. "Thank you, Cullen."

"No need to thank me. All I want is for you and Ryan to be safe."

"What about Gil?"

"They sent someone over to his house to find out."

She released a breath. "When are you coming home?"

"So you missed me?" he asked, and she heard the laughter in his voice.

"Yes, Sheriff, I missed you."

"I'm trying my damnedest to get a plane out late tonight. If I do, I'm coming straight to you. So don't be frightened if I show up in the middle of the night. Unless you don't want me to come by."

She wanted Cullen Brannigan more than she could imagine wanting anyone. That still frightened her a little. "Yes, Sheriff, please come by when you get home."

Chapter Eighteen

Cullen was exhausted by the time he pulled into the driveway. He checked the dashboard clock to see it was just after 1:00 a.m. He should go to his house. Yet, the need to see Shelby was overwhelming. He wanted to hold her when he told her everything that had happened in the past twenty-four hours. Even he had trouble comprehending all of it.

The good thing was now she'd be able to move on with her life. A life he wanted to be a part of.

It had been a long time since he believed in happily-ever-after. And he couldn't imagine that happening without Shelby. He turned off the engine. There were so many things he still needed to deal with. Find a permanent job, for one.

The second, was he the man for Shelby? Could he be the father Ryan needed? He didn't know the answer to those questions, only that he'd never felt this way about a woman before. And he wanted to see her right this minute.

His heart pounded in his chest as he walked up to the cottage, but before he could knock, the door swung open and Shelby appeared. He dropped his bag as she rushed into his arms. His kiss nearly devoured her, leaving no doubt he wanted her.

The feeling of her sweet body against him drove away

every doubt as these new feelings filled his heart. He finally released her, reached down and grabbed his bag.

Once inside, he pulled her back into his arms. "So you were waiting up for me?"

"You could say that." She stepped back. "I also wanted to find out what happened with Gil."

He placed a finger against her lips. The last thing he wanted was to spoil this homecoming. "Let's hold off any business talk until later." He closed the space between them. "I want to focus on you right now."

"What do you have in mind, Sheriff?" Her voice was low and sultry.

"Let me show you."

He took her hand and led her down the hall to her dimly lit bedroom. Inside he closed the door quietly, and he pulled her back into his arms. "Damn, woman. You have no idea how much I missed you."

She pressed her body against his. "I've missed you, too. I'm so glad you're back."

Trying to hold himself in check, he softly brushed his mouth across hers, once, twice and a third time. "I'm pretty glad, too."

Then he heard her whispered plea. "I need you, Cullen. So much."

That set everything in motion, and his mouth crushed hers, his hunger taking over, and his hands tugged at her robe. Once it was stripped away, he cupped her breasts through her thin gown, drawing a soft whimper from her. Soon, he tugged the tiny straps from her shoulders and down her arms. He took a needed breath as he gazed on her perfect form.

"So beautiful." He leaned down and captured her nipple in his mouth and gently sucked until the pebble hardened against his tongue.

Shelby gasped as the sensation nearly drove her over the edge. She gripped his arms for support. "Oh, Cullen…"

He released her and began to strip off his shirt. "I want you, Shelby." Next he worked his boots off, then his trousers. "Now." His mouth closed over hers, and Shelby couldn't think any longer, nor did she want to.

Once naked, Cullen came back to her and slipped her gown the rest of the way off, then he laid her down onto the bed. Heart pounding, she stared at the man leaning over her. She placed her palms against his broad chest, then ran them down his muscular arms. Suddenly she needed to feel his power all around her.

"Make love to me, Cullen."

A smile broke out on his face as he lowered his body over hers. "I plan to," he whispered.

She wrapped her arms around him as he slipped deep inside her, and together they rode out the crest until they reached heaven.

In the quiet hours before dawn, Shelby could still feel the euphoria of their joining. She rolled over and laid her arm across Cullen's waist. "I'm so glad you're home." She kissed his bare chest and felt his shiver.

"I kind of got that idea." His hand caressed her back. "Maybe I should leave more often."

She raised her head. "No. I mean, if you need to, of course." She knew it was a real possibility that he might be leaving soon. "I know the sheriff's job is ending soon, but I hope you find something close by."

"So you like me hanging around, huh?"

She decided she needed to be honest with him. "Yes, but I think you already know that." She glanced away, needing to tell him her future plans. "Bess and Bill offered to sell me All Occasions Catering."

He froze.

"They made me a generous offer *making* it possible for me to buy it."

"So you told them yes?"

"More or less, but I haven't signed any papers." She propped her chin up on her hands. "I want to make my home here with Ryan permanent. It's important he have some stability."

Cullen was quiet for a long time, and it was Shelby who spoke up. "This is your home, too, Cullen. You're part owner in this ranch."

"A ranch that doesn't make any money. I'm not a cattleman like Trent. I've been in law enforcement since college, but there isn't anything here. As soon as Sheriff Carson comes back, I'm out of a job. I need to find work."

Cullen scooted up and leaned against the headboard, then he pulled her back into his arms. He had hoped that if he couldn't find anything close by, that she might consider moving with him. "I heard the police department is hiring in Grand Junction."

He felt her tense against him.

He continued to say, "I know it's asking a lot, but I was hoping we could work something out. I care about you, Shelby. I want to be with you and Ryan. But so far, I haven't come up with anything in this town." He had had a few other ideas about a security system, but he'd have to invest a lot of money into equipment. "I'm not sure what I'm going to do. I have some ideas that I'm mulling around."

She reached for his hand, and laced her fingers with his. "Seems that when we get one problem solved, another pops up."

He brought her hand to his lips and kissed it. He thought back to last year when he'd been fighting for his career, his life. He never wanted to go back, but he hadn't moved forward, either. And he couldn't until he decided what he wanted out of life before he asked Shelby to share it.

"I don't see being here with you right now a problem."

He felt her body against his, and he desired her once again. As much as he wanted to lose himself in her, he had some thinking to do.

"I should be going before Ryan comes rushing in here." He released her, got out of bed and slipped on his pants. Then he pulled his henley shirt over his head. He made the mistake of looking at Shelby on the bed, and he resisted the urge to go back to her.

"Wait, you never told me what happened with Gil." She looked worried. "Will we have to go back to Kentucky to testify?"

Cullen sat down on the bed. "No, your testimony isn't needed. Gil decided he didn't want to face his crimes, and before the police could get to his house…he took his own life."

She gasped. "He's dead?"

Cullen nodded. "You'll probably hear from Captain Kershaw later this morning, but you'll never have to go back there, unless you want to."

She shook her head. "I can't believe it. He can't hurt us anymore."

Cullen slipped his arm around her shoulders. "No, he can't. You and Ryan are safe now."

She raised her head. "I'm sorry that a person lost his life, but I'm not sorry that this nightmare is finally over." Tears filled her eyes, and she wiped them away. "Now we can truly move on from the past."

Cullen pulled her back into his arms. He wished he could offer her everything her heart desired. But he wasn't sure of his own future yet, so how could he promise her anything? He had to figure a way to change that.

THE NEXT DAY, Cullen went to work, but all he'd managed to do was think about Shelby. How much he wanted to be a part of her and Ryan's lives. That meant he had to figure out a way to make a living here.

He drove his truck up beside the house and saw his dad in the corral with the horses. And there was his father to consider. It had been nearly a month since Neal Brannigan showed up at his door. Cullen smiled. Strange, he didn't want to think about Dad not being here.

After changing out of his sheriff's uniform, Cullen went out to the barn, where he found his father was mucking out a stall.

"Hey, you don't need to do that."

Neal looked over his shoulder. "Just earning my keep."

"Dad, you don't need to earn anything. I should ask Trent about sending one of his hands over to help out."

Neal leaned against his rake. "Actually, I enjoy doing this."

"Okay, I'll help then."

It took about an hour, but they managed to finish up the rest of the stalls. They went inside the house for a quick sandwich, and Cullen suggested they go on a ride.

Cullen saddled the chestnut, Danny Boy, and met his father in the corral on the bay gelding, Dakota. They left the other horses in the fenced pasture to graze and run, then took off toward the foothills.

They rode at an easy pace, and Cullen was able to enjoy the Colorado spring flora and fauna. A jackrabbit hopped across the trail. Yellow and blue wildflowers covered the prairie, and reminded him of Shelby.

She was different, down-home and creative, and loving and caring…

His father's voice broke through his reverie. "You're daydreaming, son. Wouldn't be about a certain woman, would it?"

He nodded. "That's what I wanted to talk to you about."

Neal leaned an arm on his saddle horn. "If you want me to move out of the house, that's not a problem."

"No, Dad. I don't want you to go. In fact, I hope you'll stay…for as long as you want."

He gave his son a sideways glance. "I don't want to be in the way."

"You're not in the way. So get that out of your head. You've been a big help with the ranch. All these horses need care, but I don't want you having to muck out stalls. Like I said, Trent offered to send over one of his men a few times a week."

"There are only four horses to care for. I can handle them on my own."

"Okay, but promise me you'll say something if it gets to be too much."

"I will." His father glanced at him. "There is something I wanted to speak to you about. Jeanie Phelps called this morning. The word has gotten around about her sons coming out here. She knows a few other mothers who would like to bring their special-needs kids to ride, too."

"I guess we could plan another day. How many kids?"

His dad was quiet for a moment. "I had an idea we could do this on a more permanent basis. If we had a few more horses and tack, maybe another special saddle to handle the severally handicapped kids."

Cullen held up his hand. "Whoa. We only have four horses and there're only a few of us."

"The horses might not be a problem. A man stopped

by yesterday while you were in Kentucky. He has two… mature horses he wants to donate to the program."

"Program? Dad, do you realize what we'll be getting into?"

Neal looked him in the eyes. "Yes. Jeanie's been doing some research. We need to charge a fee, but if some parents can't afford it, then of course we can help them out. Jeannie even talked with Haskell's Feed Store. Ben has offered to donate some of the feed and some bales of straw." Neal shifted in his saddle. "His grandson has autism, and he thinks the program is a great idea."

They started moving again, and the slow, easy rocking in the saddle had Cullen thinking of possibilities. "What about volunteers? We can't do this all alone. Did Jeanie come up with any ideas?"

His dad nodded. "That woman is a force to be reckoned with. Her idea is to get high school kids who need community-service hours to graduate. I'm not going to pressure you, son. I'll let you think about it. Just so you know, Jeanie and I will handle most of the work. Of course, if you're not working for the sheriff's office, it would be nice if you'd participate."

"That's what I wanted to talk to you about. My contract is up in two weeks, and I need to find something else. I might not have a choice but to leave town."

His father grew serious. "There's always a choice, son. Take it from one who knows. I made a lot of wrong ones and I missed out on so much. Make your priorities, and your career shouldn't always be on the top of that list." His father looked sad, then brightened again. "And there aren't many women like Shelby out there."

"I know that, Dad." He blew out a breath. "If I didn't care so much about her and Ryan, this wouldn't be so hard."

"Then find a way to stay here," his father stressed. "Talk with Trent and see what you can come up with."

They were nearly back to the barn when Shelby's car pulled in. His heart raced at the chance to see her again. Ryan climbed out of the backseat and ran toward the corral. The boy knew the rules with the horses, and he went to the ramp to meet them.

"Hi, Cullen. Hi, Pops."

"Hi, Ryan." His father swung Ryan up in front of him on the horse. Without a question, the boy took the reins and kicked Dakota's sides, and they walked off.

Cullen had his gaze on Shelby as she walked over to the fence. He swung his leg over the horse and jumped down. Once she reached him, he drew her close and kissed her, wishing they were alone so he could do it properly.

"I missed you today," he said, not releasing her.

"I missed you, too," she said, but her gaze didn't quite meet his.

"Is something wrong?"

She shook here head. "No, just a long day."

"Then let me take you out for dinner. I know Dad will stay with Ryan so you and I can talk about…things."

She shook her head. "Would you mind if we make it another time? I'm really tired. I brought leftovers home from the café. I just want to shower, put on pj's and watch a movie with Ryan. Sorry. I'm not good company tonight."

He hid his disappointment. "I understand. Why don't you go to the cottage, and I'll drop off Ryan after his ride?"

She finally smiled. "Thanks for understanding." She turned and walked off.

The problem was he did understand. She wanted what he hadn't been able to offer her. Permanence. She deserved a man who could give her that.

Chapter Nineteen

Later that evening, Cullen sat at Trent and Brooke's kitchen table, discussing his idea. "And that's the plan."

Trent frowned. "You know how to install and run all this equipment?"

Cullen nodded. "It's what I did the last five years on the police force."

Trent tipped his chair back and grinned. "So you're some sort of computer whiz?"

"Maybe. Mainly, I know how to install security equipment. And from what I've seen around town, there are several businesses who need to do a better job protecting their property. Better security will help their insurance rates, too."

Trent sat up straight. "So where do you want to go with this?"

"I want to start up a business, specializing in security cameras that I design and build. I could do ranches, too. I mean, Laurel has some pretty valuable horses at the Rawlins Ranch."

Trent arched an eyebrow. "Do you need some money to start up?"

Cullen shook his head. "No, I have money from my settlement from the police department. I plan to start small, so for now, I'll probably set up my office at the ranch. Maybe I'll use the garage for the equipment storage, and the room upstairs for my command center. But since it's partly your ranch, too, I don't want to take over the entire place."

Trent leaned forward. "How about this? Brooke and I talked it over and decided that I would sign the Circle R Ranch over to you and Austin."

Cullen shook his head. "No! You can't give it to us. The land is too valuable."

"Okay, here's another idea. I'll take two sections of the grazing land that borders the Lucky Bar L Ranch. That way you get the houses and outbuildings. Especially now that Neal wants to start the therapy riding center."

"That's still very generous of you, Trent."

His stepbrother grinned. "I know, but how else am I going to get my brothers to stay here?" He sobered. "Look Cullen, it took me a lot of years away in the military to realize what's important. It's family. And I'm hoping you're smart enough to include Shelby in these plans."

"Now that she's not a flight risk, I plan to keep her and Ryan here permanently."

Brooke walked into the kitchen. "If Shelby loves you, she'll back you."

Trent reached for his wife and pulled her down onto his lap. "The right woman will get you to change a lot of plans, or to make plans."

Brooke smiled. "You're the one who chased me to Vegas and brought me back here."

He kissed her. "And I'd do it again. I didn't want to live without you."

"And I don't want to live without Shelby and Ryan," Cullen added.

The phone began to ring, interrupting their conversation. Trent answered it and walked out of the room.

Minutes later he was back. "That was the head of the city council. It seems that Ted Carson has decided to retire." He looked at Cullen. "It seems you have another option, brother."

LATER THAT NIGHT, Shelby couldn't sleep. When that happened, she usually started planning. Her day...her money...her life...

She looked down at the list on the paper. If she took Bess and Bill's offer, she still had to make payments to them, and she'd like it paid off the sooner the better. She didn't want to be beholden to anyone. That was how her grandmother raised her.

Don't take handouts unless there isn't any choice.

This wasn't a handout. This was a business deal, and a good investment for her. It was a future for her and Ryan. And maybe in a year or so, she could even open a bakery at the catering center when Ryan was in school. Then she'd have a second income.

She looked around at the cottage. This was the best home she'd had in so long, or maybe just because of the connection to Cullen. She smiled. His family was pretty great, too.

She sighed. Sometimes you had to be practical with relationships, especially when the man wouldn't be around. If she kept living here when Cullen went off to Grand Junction, would he feel obligated to her?

She thought about last night and the man's incredible loving. There was no doubt that Cullen cared about her. And she was definitely head over heels in love with the handsome sheriff.

Yet, sometimes dreams never come true. She thought of her sister, and her chest tightened. It wasn't fair that she and Georgia never got to have more time together.

That a mother never got to raise her son. She wiped away a tear. Oh, God. She missed her big sister so much. But she couldn't forget about Ryan. She promised Georgia that she'd give him a good home and love him as if he were her own son.

She smiled. Loving Ryan was the easy part.

There was a soft knock on the door. She got up and looked out the peephole to see Cullen. Her heart raced at the thought of being with him. She opened the door a crack.

"Cullen."

He frowned at her. "I know you said you wanted to have an early night, but I had to see you."

She wanted to see him, too. "I need to be at work early." She hated fibbing to him. "So could we talk tomorrow?"

"This is important, Shelby." He stepped closer and she tried to back up, but he reached for her. "But I need to do this first." He lowered his head, and his mouth covered hers.

Shelby didn't have a chance to stop him, and once his lips touched hers, she didn't want to. She needed this man more than her next breath. She wrapped her arms around him and let him deepen the kiss.

Finally she broke away and stepped back. "Look, Cullen, if this is what you came for, I don't think I can handle it. You're going to be leaving us, and I feel that it would be best if we didn't spend so much time together."

She walked away, then turned around. This was strange because she was usually the one to leave. Now, she wanted to stay, and the guy was going.

Cullen saw the pain on her face, and he wanted to tell her that he wasn't going away. "Shelby, just listen."

"No, I can't listen anymore. I have Ryan to think about now. He doesn't need to be torn away from more people. I don't want to lose any more people, either. I've lived on the outside for so long, and can't do it anymore. I want more. I deserve more." She forced a smile. "You're so wonderful, Cullen, and I hope you find the life you want, but I'm staying put, because I worked hard to build a life right here."

He walked to her, hoping he could come up with the right words he needed to say. "You're special to me, Shelby, and so is Ryan. I want you to have your dream. I only hope you have some room in that life for me, too."

He took a needed breath. "I've been trying to outrun my past as if I did something wrong. I didn't lie, cheat or steal anything. I've been exonerated. I'll never go back to Denver, but I realized I hadn't moved on, either. Well, I'm doing it now, by staying put right here."

Seeing the surprised look on her face, he reached for her hand and felt her trembling. "Shelby Townsend, I want you and Ryan in my life. I want you to build that catering business, and I want to help." He pulled her close. "I love you, Shelby. I want to share that life right here in Hidden Springs."

She blinked. "Oh, Cullen. I love you, too."

"Good." He kissed her quick and hard. "Then it's settled."

"Wait a minute. What about your job? Aren't you going to Grand Junction?"

He shook his head. "I don't need to. There seem to be a couple of jobs here that I qualify for. Ted Carson decided to retire. Trent told me tonight. He's on the town council, so he offered me the job, at least until the next election."

He watched her blue eyes widen. "Really?"

He nodded. "But it gets better. I have an idea about a security business." He went on to tell her about his plans as he drew her close. "I was trying to think of a way to stay here. God, Shelby, I didn't want to leave you. I never want to leave you."

He stepped back. "I know this isn't the way a woman likes it done, but I can't wait." He went to one knee, his chest tight with so many emotions. "Shelby Townsend, I love you with all my heart. I can't imagine not having you in my life. I love Ryan so much. I hope one day I can adopt him so he'll be mine, too. Will you marry me and live right here on this ranch?"

Tears filled her eyes as she opened her mouth to speak.

"Say, yes, Aunt Shellie."

They both turned to see Ryan standing in the doorway, a big grin on his face.

Shelby waved him over to her. He ran to her. "So you want us to marry the sheriff?"

The boy nodded. "Yes. I want him to be my dad."

Cullen had to swallow hard as he waited for Shelby to end his agony. Yet, seeing the love in her eyes, he wasn't worried. "Take one more chance, Shelby. I promise, I'll be there for you. I'm not leaving you. Ever."

She leaned down and said, "Yes, we'll marry you."

He heard the boy cheer, but Cullen stood and wrapped his arms around his woman. "I love you." He covered her mouth in a kiss that he hoped told her how much. How much he wanted them to be a family, to build together what had eluded them all. Not any longer. They could do anything, together. He pulled back and scooped up Ryan in his arms. "So you want us to get married?"

Ryan nodded. "And have babies, too."

They both laughed. Cullen was the first to sober, and said, "So you want a little sister or brother?"

"Yes. One girl and one boy."

Shelby smiled. "I think I can handle that."

Cullen leaned down and kissed her. "And you know I'll do my part." He winked. "We're a family, Shelby. And don't you forget it."

Epilogue

It was a sunny June day. Perfect for the grand opening of Georgia's Therapy Riding Center. Shelby stood back with her camera and watched as the group of parents, along with their children, gathered around the ramp for the ribbon cutting. Pops and Cullen stood on either side of Ryan, who held a pair of big scissors. With help, her nephew cut the ribbon, and cheers erupted.

She'd never get tired of watching Cullen with Ryan. The love and patience the man showed for the five-year-old made her heart swell with love. As if it were possible to love him more.

She watched the first group of kids as they mounted their horses. High school volunteers assisted all the kids, spotting them during the ride, and cared for the animals in the barn. Shelby knew that Pops was the strong force behind the volunteers, making sure they were serious about their jobs. Four more horses had been donated, Daisy, Clancy, Taffy and Bandit. They'd been lucky that all the horses were well behaved and loved being around kids.

Trent, Kase and Laurel came to help out because of the extra people today. Neal officially ran the center, and they planned to be open two days a week, Tuesday and Thursday afternoons, from the spring to the fall.

Jeanie was a big help, too. She made sure there were

adult volunteers, including the sheriff's deputies who were here today. Great public relations.

So many of the townspeople showed up to offer support for the program, and for their sheriff, too. Cullen had become a pretty popular figure in the town. He'd kept the position as sheriff for now, at least until the election in eighteen months. Hopefully by then his business, Brannigan Security, would take off, and if it did, he wouldn't run for the office. He wanted to spend more time with his family.

Shelby had to concentrate on her catering business, too. And she'd been busy, especially since she'd been planning her and Cullen's wedding. Luckily, it was a small one, with only family and some friends attending at the Q and L Guest Lodge in July. Then she and Ryan would move in to the house, and Pops would take over the cottage.

Shelby felt a hand on her shoulder and turned around to see Cullen. He pulled her into his arms and kissed her. She got the familiar rush whenever he touched her.

Aware of people around, she pulled back. "Why aren't you with the kids?"

"Not needed with so many volunteers." He pointed to the arena. "Besides, this is Dad's show." He turned back to her. "I wanted to know if you needed some help."

She shrugged. "Judy and Corey are doing a great job." She glanced at the long table filled with food. A banner advertising her catering business was draped on the table as her new teenage hires dished out food. So far they had been a great help to her at the weekend receptions.

They'd also set up a raffle table to win a free weekend stay at the Q and L Guest Lodge, with all proceeds going to the riding center.

Cullen pulled Shelby close to his side. He didn't like

her too far away. They'd both worked too hard to get here, to find each other, and he never wanted her to doubt his love.

"I can't believe this turnout," he said.

"Word gets around in a small town. We're blessed to have so many friends and family."

"And I'm blessed to have you and Ryan." He kissed her, and whistles filled the air. "I guess we better continue this in private. Later." He took off and went back to the arena, thinking about later when they had time to themselves and he could show her how much he loved her.

ON A WARM July afternoon, Shelby came out of the upstairs guestrooms at the Q and L Guest Lodge on her wedding day. With one last look, she checked her long, ivory lace and satin wedding gown. She felt her eyes mist as she stroked the fabric lovingly. She was blessed that her cousin's wife had heard of her upcoming nuptials and contacted her about Grandma's ivory wedding dress she'd found in the attic at the farm. And on this, her special day, Shelby felt her family was with her.

She touched the gold chain that held Georgia's sapphire teardrop pendant, which she'd borrowed for today. Then she would put it away for Ryan's bride. She wore no veil, only flowers woven in her updo-styled hair. She carried the same simple flowers as in her bouquet.

"You look pretty, Aunt Shellie."

She smiled at the boy in the tux, his curly blond hair combed neatly, and his face scrubbed clean of any traces of peanut butter. She'd come to love this child more than she could ever imagine. "Thank you. I think you look pretty handsome, too. You ready to get married?"

He nodded. "Yes, 'cause Cullen's gonna be my new dad, but I don't have to forget my other dad. Cullen said so."

Her chest tightened with emotion. "I think we're pretty lucky to have Cullen." And she couldn't wait to become his wife.

She looked up when Brooke Landry called to her. Her matron of honor walked toward her dressed in a long sheath-style gown of pale blue.

"The music started, so that's our cue," Brooke said.

"Let's go." She took Ryan's arm and they headed down the open staircase to the large main room where their family and friends sat on either side of a long white runner. At the end stood her handsome groom dressed in a black tux. There was a large picture window and in the background the majestic mountains.

Her heart pounded in her chest as she somehow made her way up the aisle to Cullen. She kept focused on his hazel eyes. Next to him was Neal, smiling at her.

Once they arrived, the minister asked, "Who gives this woman away in matrimony?"

Ryan raised his hand. "I do."

Snickers of laughter moved through the group as he went and stood beside Pops.

Cullen couldn't take his eyes off his beautiful bride. He was mesmerized as he took her hand and kissed it, then leaned forward and whispered, "Glad you could make it."

She squeezed back. "I wouldn't miss it for the world."

He blew out a breath, trying to calm his racing heart, but the condition seemed to be permanent whenever he was around this woman. Somehow he managed to pull himself together and focus on their vows.

A few minutes later, the minister said, "I now pronounce you husband and wife. You may kiss your bride."

"This is what I've been waiting for." He lowered his

head and tasted her sweet lips. Once he pulled back, he said, "Hello, Mrs. Brannigan."

She smiled. "I like the sound of that."

"Get used to it, because you're stuck with me for at least the next fifty or sixty years."

They faced their guests as the minister announced, "I'd like to present to you, Mr. and Mrs. Cullen Brannigan."

"Yay!" Ryan cheered. "We're married."

Cullen took the boy's hand as did Shelby, and they walked down the aisle as a family. He began to count his blessings, recalling the night that he found Shelby and Ryan in his house. That night his dark life began to brighten.

Sometimes you never find what you're looking for, and sometimes…you're lucky enough to have that someone find you. He reached for his bride and pulled her close. And you get to go on the journey together.

* * * * *

MILLS & BOON®

Cherish™

EXPERIENCE THE ULTIMATE RUSH OF FALLING IN LOVE

A sneak peek at next month's titles...

In stores from 12th January 2017:

- **The Sheikh's Convenient Princess** – Liz Fielding *and*
  His Pregnant Courthouse Bride – Rachel Lee
- **The Billionaire of Coral Bay** – Nikki Logan *and*
  Baby Talk & Wedding Bells – Brenda Harlen

In stores from 26th January 2017:

- **Her First-Date Honeymoon** – Katrina Cudmore *and*
  Falling for the Rebound Bride – Karen Templeton
- **The Unforgettable Spanish Tycoon** – Meg Maxwell
  and **Her Sweetest Fortune** – Stella Bagwell

Just can't wait?
Buy our books online a month before they hit the shops!
www.millsandboon.co.uk

Also available as eBooks.

MILLS & BOON®

EXCLUSIVE EXTRACT

Sheikh Ibrahim al-Ansari must find a bride,
and quickly... Thankfully he has the perfect
convenient princess in mind—his new assistant,
Ruby Dance!

Read on for a sneak preview of
THE SHEIKH'S CONVENIENT PRINCESS
by Liz Fielding

'Can I ask if you are in any kind of relationship?' he
persisted.

'Relationship?'

'You are on your own—you have no ties?'

He was beginning to spook her and must have realised
it because he said, 'I have a proposition for you, Ruby,
but if you have personal commitments...' He shook his
head as if he wasn't sure what he was doing.

'If you're going to offer me a package too good to
refuse after a couple of hours I should warn you that it
took Jude Radcliffe the best part of a year to get to that
point and I still turned him down.'

'I don't have the luxury of time,' he said, 'and the
position I'm offering is made for a temp.'

'I'm listening.'

'Since you have done your research, you know that
I was disinherited five years ago.'

She nodded. She thought it rather harsh for a one-off

incident but the media loved the fall of a hero and had gone into a bit of a feeding frenzy.

'This morning I received a summons from my father to present myself at his birthday majlis.'

'You can go home?'

'If only it were that simple. A situation exists which means that I can only return to Umm al Basr if I'm accompanied by a wife.'

She ignored the slight sinking feeling in her stomach. Obviously a multimillionaire who looked like the statue of a Greek god—albeit one who'd suffered a bit of wear and tear—would have someone ready and willing to step up to the plate.

'That's rather short notice. Obviously, I'll do whatever I can to arrange things, but I don't know a lot about the law in—'

'The marriage can take place tomorrow. My question is, under the terms of your open-ended brief encompassing "whatever is necessary", are you prepared to take on the role?'

Don't miss
THE SHEIKH'S CONVENIENT PRINCESS
By Liz Fielding

Available February 2017
www.millsandboon.co.uk

Give a 12 month subscription to a friend today!

Call Customer Services
0844 844 1358*

or visit
millsandboon.co.uk/subscriptions